THE KILLING

A BETH PAPADAKIS THRILLER

CARA ALEXANDER

This is a work of fiction. Names, characters, organizations, places, events, and incidents are either products of the author's imagination or used fictitiously.

EXCLUSIVE OFFER

Look out for the link at the end of this book or visit my website at www.caraaalexander.com to sign up to my no-spam VIP Club and received a FREE prequel to the Beth Papadakis series plus news and previews of new books.

Never miss a new release.

No spam, ever, guaranteed. You can unsubscribe at any time.

ALSO BY CARA ALEXANDER

Followed

Panic

Payback

Pure Evil

Fallout

PROLOGUE

Athens, Greece

4 February, 10.15pm in the evening...

'We need to meet. All I want is a few minutes of your time.'

James doesn't know who the man is or why he's calling him, and he's getting pissed off.

'You won't tell me your name, so why should I bother?'

'It's urgent,' the rasping Greek voice hisses. 'It's a matter of life and death. You can stop someone from being killed. You must come!' He lowers his voice, just a little. 'Do you know Fanis Bar, in Glyfada? It's off the main highway, the bar with the terrace outside?'

James says something, but the Greek carries on.

'I'll be there at 10.30, be there.'

Then he hangs up.

James stands staring at his phone. *Is the guy mad or just winding me up?*

Gulping down the rest of the coffee he's just bought from the cafe across the square, he crumples the now empty polystyrene cup into a ball, tosses it into a nearby bin, then crosses the road to a small side street where his car's parked.

All he wants is to go home, have a beer, put his feet up, but he can't—he arranged to meet Helen. She said it was urgent so he can't let her down.

He clicks his key fob, the car springs into action.

His phone rings - number withheld.

James stares at his phone.

Is it that crazy Greek again?

'Yes,' he snaps.

'I want you to understand how important this is. It is of international concern. This man's life is in danger. We must do something to stop it.'

Oh my God, the guy just doesn't give up, but for some strange reason, James has a gut feeling about this. It could be the scoop of a lifetime. He might be wrong, but what if the guy is telling the truth?

'Okay, but it'd better be good. What do you look like?'

The man sighs with relief. 'I'm wearing a brown velvet jacket and a striped scarf.'

'I'll be there in about fifteen minutes,' James mutters.

He slides into his car, switches on the air con and calls Helen to say he'll be a little late.

She sounds irritated but agrees to wait for him. She knows if he has a bee in his bonnet about a story, there's no stopping him.

Ten minutes later, he's out of the center of Athens, heading towards the upmarket beachside resort of Glyfada. As usual, Posseidonas Avenue is busy; it's the main coastal road leading to other popular beachside resorts and also leads to Cape Sounion and the ruins of the Temple of Poseidon.

The neon lights of the restaurants and hotels shed a

rainbow of colours over the highway that remind him of when he worked in London, clandestine meetings like this are now a thing of the past. He smiles to himself—that's probably why he agreed to see the guy.

Putting his foot down hard on the accelerator, he urges his old car to go faster. Before moving to Athens, he'd worked as a journalist, but when his friend Beth invited him to her wedding in Athens, his whole life changed.

Within a matter of weeks, he'd handed in his notice, packed up his stuff in London, moved to Athens, and started a part-time job at a local college teaching English. Thanks to an uncle's inheritance, he now owns a small delicatessen in Athens, and works part time as a journalist.

He slows down; he doesn't want to miss the turning, it's around here somewhere. Drivers honk their horns in frustration as he edges the car over to the inside lane. On leaving the highway, he turns left into a tree-lined street leading to *Fanis Bar*. Out of the corner of his eye, he can see the guy—it must be him—he's the only one on the terrace. He's sitting with his legs crossed on an old rickety looking chair, nonchalantly smoking a cigarette.

James sits for a few seconds, watching him. The guy's probably in his 40s or 50s, with longish brown hair and a thin moustache. There's a small glass of something in front of him which he picks up and slowly drinks, then he puts the glass down and draws deeply on his cigarette. He does this a few times, then looks around, probably wondering where James is.

Without bothering to lock the car door, James walks quickly up the couple of steps to the open bar terrace.

The man sees him, waves his hand and beckons him over. His dark eyes rest on James's face for a second, then he looks away. 'What will you drink?' he asks, flicking the ash off of his cigarette into the ashtray.

James pulls out another rickety looking chair opposite the Greek. 'A beer, thanks.'

The waiter leans against the open bar door smoking a cigarette, watching them. The Greek glances over at him and points to James.

'*Mia bira parakalo.*'

The waiter nods, takes another drag of his cigarette, flicks it into the night air and saunters inside the bar.

James leans back in his chair and studies the man opposite him. The Greek returns his gaze.

'So, what do you want to tell me?' James asks.

The Greek leans forward, slightly. 'I have some news that will shock you.' He stops for a minute, glances around at the nearby tables, then, as if satisfied, carries on talking. 'You must tell no one what I'm about to tell you—if you do, your life and mine will be in danger.' James nods, the Greek carries on. 'I can't tell you everything tonight. We will meet in a few days, in another place, and then I will tell you more. We must be careful, you understand?'

James raises an eyebrow. He sits watching the Greek, trying to fathom him out. He looks like an actor or he could be a teacher. It all sounds dramatic, but hey, this is the land where Greek drama flourished in the late sixth century BC.

The man sits holding his gaze, his dark eyes defiant.

Suddenly James smiles. 'Don't worry, you can trust me.'

The man draws hard on his cigarette, blows a circle of smoke into the night air and leans closer to James. 'I have this on very good authority. They intend to kidnap the Prime Minister and kill him.' He looks at James intently, as if waiting for a reaction. James says nothing, so the Greek carries on. 'At the moment, he's popular with some Greeks, but many want him out of the way.'

James sits looking at him, wondering if the guy's for real, or just some crazy academic who's finally cracked. He could well understand this happening—the economy is recovering, but many Greeks are still suffering, thousands have left the country and those that remain are very rich or struggling to make ends meet.

He sits watching the man opposite him with interest. Just like many Greeks, he smokes too much and always seems to be thinking. James shifts in his chair and scratches his head. If it's true what he says, then he needs to know more, much more. Maybe his friend Dev is the person the man should speak to? This is his line of work and he has the necessary contacts.

James frowns. 'I'll have to discuss this with one of my colleagues—he has experience in this sort of thing—I also need to know who's behind this, when it's going to happen and where?'

The Greek's eyes narrow. 'How do I know I can trust your friend? What is his name?'

James looks at him in surprise. Does the guy really expect him to tell him?

'If he agrees to help, then I'll tell you his name, but don't worry, he's one of the best.' As an afterthought, he adds. 'You haven't told me your name?'

The man's silent then waves his hand in the air dismissively, the way Greeks do—he lights another cigarette—his eyes never leave James's face. 'My name doesn't matter.'

James leans back in his chair and stares at him. 'Why all the secrecy? Who are you?'

'My name doesn't matter. I prefer it this way.'

James shifts in his chair, the guy's beginning to irritate

him. 'What about my phone number? How did you get that?'

The Greek smiles, slightly. 'It was easy. I went to your food shop. I told the Spanish woman working there I was an old friend of yours, that I needed to speak to you—I said it was very urgent and she told me.'

James's wife Isabelle often works in the delicatessen when it's busy, or when he's out. He's lost count of the times he's asked her not to give anyone his number.

Running his hand through his hair, he surveys the man opposite him. 'It makes no sense—why choose me when there are so many Greek journalists who would jump at a scoop like this?'

The Greek shrugs his shoulders and looks at him. 'I read your newspaper articles. I know how you think. I've checked you out.' Then, as an afterthought, he adds. 'I have to be careful.'

The waiter saunters over, flicks the table with a red cloth, places a glass of beer in front of James, then walks back to the open bar door and lights a cigarette.

James sips the ice-cold beer, relishing the Moorish taste of the amber liquid. He sits watching the Greek for a few minutes. In a way, he's enjoying the drama of the situation—he just wishes his friend Dev was here, this is his line of work.

In his shirt pocket is a hundred-euro bill he keeps for occasions like this.

He reaches inside his pocket, then stops.

Maybe the Greek will want more?

As if reading his mind, the Greek waves his hand. 'I don't want your money. I just want you to take this seriously. We must stop them before...'

James nods. 'Yes, before they kill him.'

The Greek sits watching him. James drains his beer, then glances at his phone. It's getting late, he must hurry, Helen will be there soon.

He leans forward and picks up his car keys. 'When do you think this will happen?'

The man looks surprised. 'If I knew, I would tell you, but it won't be long. I might find out more tonight, but you must promise not to repeat what I have said, otherwise...'

He makes a gesture across his neck.

'Don't worry, this is between you and me. I'll wait for your call.'

The man nods.

James stands up to go.

There's the sound of shooting.

Everything goes black for James.

The headlines on the Athens tabloid press the following morning read:

SHOOTING IN ATHENS BEACH BAR LATE THIS EVENING - ONE DEAD, ONE ON LIFE SUPPORT IN HOSPITAL

1

ELIAS

Athens, 5 February
11.00 pm

The office buzzes with life like any other city newspaper on a weekday night.

With a sigh of relief Elias closes his laptop, he leaves the office, strides towards the elevator and presses the button to go down. The thought of an ice-cold beer on his veranda at home makes him lick his dry lips.

'Elias, come back!'

Oh no! Now what!

Stavros, the chief editor is standing at the office door looking at him excitedly. 'Come and see what's just come in!'

Elias dutifully returns to the office and stands staring at the huge computer screen on Stavros's desk.

The newsflash reads - SHOOTING IN GLYFADA BEACH BAR.

Elias raises his eyebrows; he knows what's coming.

Stavros points to the screen. 'On your way home, make a detour, find out what's happening, we can get this in the early morning edition if you hurry.'

Elias nods, what can he say, they're already short of staff and this looks big. 'Is the photographer there,' he asks, turning to leave the room.

'He's on his way, call me when you get there, now hurry.'

It's nearly midnight by the time Elias reaches the scene of the shooting. Police tape cordons off the small side street from the main highway where the bar's located.

In front of the shattered bar window, shards of glass lay strewn across the terrace. Two bodies lay twisted and still.

Onlookers stand gazing in horror at the terrible scene.

A TV film crew are in the process of setting up their lighting equipment but there's no sign of Elias's photographer.

With his pass showing, he ducks under the police tape and peers at a paramedic standing nearby. 'Are they alive?'

The paramedic points to a stretcher being taken away.

'This one might stand a chance, but not the other one.'

'Any idea who they are?'

The paramedic shakes his head. 'The waiter's inside, they can't get much out of him, seems he was smoking outside the bar door when it happened.'

Elias walks back towards the waiting ambulance wondering who the poor bastards are. He glances down at the blood-soaked body being carried to the ambulance and stares in horror at the man laying on the stretcher.

The paramedic's watching him and comes over. 'Are you alright, do you know him?'

Elias stands staring as if in a trance. 'It's my friend,' he groans. 'It's James.'

2

BETH

LONDON, 5 February

Early morning - 8.30 am

MY CARRY-ON LUGGAGE slithers and slides as I hurry inside Bayswater Tube station. Suddenly there's a rumbling sound. Everyone charges to scan their tickets, I run with them.

Once through the barrier, I'm carried down the stairs by this mass of people onto the train. The doors slam shut, then the train hurtles through the underground tunnels of London.

My case is between my legs, I'm squashed by people either side of me. Usually I try to avoid the horror of the London rush hour, but today I'm on an early morning flight to Greece. Yesterday's general strike in Athens caused many flights to be cancelled so I'm hoping my flight's still okay, so far it is, but these things have a habit of changing.

At Earls Court station I change to the Piccadilly line for the train to the airport. It's much faster than the other train, but even more crowded.

I'm covered from head to toe in warm winter clothes, my arms are pressed against me so there's no chance of unzipping my coat. The guy facing me is inches away from my face. At every stop more people pile in, I start feeling nauseous and close my eyes.

We must be nearly there, how many more stops?

At last a voice booms from the loudspeaker announcing we've arrived at Heathrow Airport.

In desperation I give the guy next to me a shove, retrieve my luggage from between my legs and charge up the escalators to the airport.

A cold blast of air hits me as I run the few yards to airport departures, it's strangely quiet, not a good sign. Maybe my flight's been cancelled? A quick look at my phone tells me it's still okay. I make my way through customs and check for my flight gate number.

By the time I reach the gates most people have boarded, the plane's almost full. I booked an aisle seat, I think it's the best place to sit if you're travelling alone, especially if it's a long flight.

Across the aisle from me is a young Greek guy, his eyes are closed. I stow away my bag in the compartment above my seat then sit down. The two seats next to me are empty, if it stays like this I can stretch out.

No such luck, a few minutes later a young couple arrive, I stand up to let them pass to sit down, then a few minutes later we take-off.

As the plane ascends, I glance across at the small window and watch the retreating grayness of London, soon to be replaced by the blue skies and warm weather in

Athens. What luck to be sent to Greece, if only for a few days.

I settle down for the four hour flight, the young Greek guy opposite me crosses himself, the woman next to him takes a swig of something from a small bottle, she catches my eye and gives me a wink, then carries on drinking. I smile then close my eyes and start thinking of Athens.

After I've dropped my luggage off at the hotel, I'll see Helen, we're having lunch at one of our favourite restaurants. I wrap my coat around me, I'll try to sleep for a few hours, I didn't get much sleep last night. I close my eyes, I can't usually sleep when I'm travelling...

A VOICE CUTS into my dreams.

'Fasten your seat belts, please.'

I must've slept through the entire journey, I quickly sit up.

The plane begins its descent and lurches sideways, the sparkling blue Mediterranean Sea and pine topped mountains of Parnassas are visible through the small side window of the plane.

Grabbing my luggage from the overhead locker I head for the door, wait five minutes till it opens then clamber down the rickety airport steps onto the tarmac of Athens International Airport Eleftherios Venizelos.

It's hot, compared to London - 24 degrees in February is not unusual. With a surge of renewed energy, I hurry through customs then take the metro to Syntagma Square.

Fifty minutes later I'm in the very heart of Athens. Shielding my eyes from the unaccustomed sunshine, I survey the square, the open-air cafés, the old Grand Bretagne Hotel, nothing has changed.

Sighing happily, I make my way to my hotel. I'm staying at the Plaka Hotel, not as luxurious as the Grand Bretagne, but with an amazing rooftop terrace and stunning views of the Acropolis. Helen wanted me to stay at her place. If it was just Helen it would be okay, but her husband's there. As you probably guessed, I'm not a great fan of her husband.

Within minutes, I'm on Ermou Street, the main shopping district of Athens, my hotel's just a ten-minute walk from here.

When I arrive; I'm greeted like a long-lost relative. I've been here a few times before and they remember me.

My room is on the top floor, so I take the elevator, drop off my bag and ten minutes later I'm sipping an ice-cold beer on the rooftop terrace.

I give Helen a call, but it goes to voicemail, she's probably still at her meeting, I'll finish my beer, have a quick shower, then go to meet her as arranged at Mont Parnes.

3

HELEN

ATHENS, 5 February
Early morning - 8.00 am

MY PHONE'S RINGING, it must be James, we arranged to meet last night but he didn't showed up, he didn't call, which is most unlike him.

I run into my bedroom, pick up my phone from the bedside table, but it's not James, it's my husband, Theo, he didn't come home last night.

'I thought you would be at work by now, Helen.' He's silent for a minute, then carries on. 'I want to use the house today I have some business to do. I'll be there in about fifteen minutes, so make sure you're out by the time I get there.'

My phone slips from my hand, then the house phone starts ringing.

'Good morning Helen, sorry to call you on your house phone but your cell phone was busy. We need to talk, it's quite urgent, can we meet at the café in the square?'

I sigh with relief, it's Dev. 'I can be there in half an hour, is that too early?'

'No, that's fine, by the way, I mean Syntagma Square, not Kolonaki Square, is that okay?'

'Yes, of course, see you soon.'

With a sigh of relief, I head for the shower, I'll be glad to get out of here.

A few minutes later, with a towel wrapped around me I peer out of the living room window at the square below, no sign of Theo, yet.

Back in the bedroom I quickly get dressed, slip on my underwear, slide on my jeans, grab a blue top from the chair then slip on a pair of flat black shoes.

I leave the house glad to have missed Theo. But on turning the corner, I freeze, it's his car, then I groan, there's a woman in the front with him. Gritting my teeth, I run past the car and down the street.

Ten minutes later I arrive at the square, Dev's sitting on the café terrace waiting for me.

'Is everything alright?' he asks, giving me a worried look as I walk over and sit down.

Talking about Theo will only make me feel worse, so I tell him about James. 'I'm okay, but I'm worried about James, I arranged to meet him last night, but he didn't show up, have you heard from him?'

He shakes his head. 'No, but I'm sure there's nothing to worry about, you know what he's like.'

'But it's not like him, Dev,' I reply, frowning. 'He'd definitely call me if he couldn't make it. As it was, I waited till the place closed...'

'You mustn't worry, you've got enough on your plate, I'm sure there's a good explanation. Now what about a drink, coffee, tea?'

'Espresso, please.'

He beckons to the waitress, orders two coffees, then looks at me. 'Did you try calling his house phone?'

I shrug, imagining what his wife would say if I did. 'I don't like phoning him at home, his wife, well, she's not very friendly.'

Just then the waitress appears with our coffees. When she's gone Dev takes an envelope from his jacket pocket and hands it to me. 'Be careful they don't fall out.'

I draw in a sharp breath, inside are photos of my husband. The first photo is of him in a restaurant with a woman. They look very friendly, too friendly. The next photo makes me gasp, it's a photo of him, he's naked, he's having sex with the woman.

Dev lights a cigarette then passes me his phone. 'There's more...it's a video.'

I take his phone and sit staring in horror at the images of my husband in front of me. He's having sex with another naked woman.

'How on earth did you get these?' I mutter, handing him back his phone and the photos.

He shrugs. 'I have my ways.'

I nod. Although I've been expecting this, it's still a shock to see him in bed with other women.

'Look, I know this must be hard.' He stops, draws hard on his cigarette then stubs it out and looks at me. 'You now have everything you need; you have grounds for divorce.'

Over the past few weeks Dev and I have become quite good friends. Dev and James are friends from way back, that's how I got to know him. This isn't really the kind of thing Dev does, so I'm lucky he agreed to help.

'Is there somewhere you can stay for a few days, till this is over?' Dev asks, breaking into my thoughts.

I shake my head. 'No, today I have a meeting with a couple of French travel agents, then I'm meeting an old friend from London. Can we talk about this tomorrow, Dev?'

'Of course, give me a ring when you're ready to discuss it.'

Before leaving my office, I try calling James, still no reply. I make my way to Syntagma Square and from there take the bus to the teleferique, it only takes seven minutes in the cable car to Mont Parness, much quicker than taking a taxi.

I force a smile to my lips as I climb the steps to the hotel entrance, then I walk over to reception to see if my potential business partners have arrived. I'm told they have, they're waiting for me in the bar.

4

BETH

ATHENS, 5 February
Later that day

AS I LEAVE the hotel the delicious aroma of fresh coffee and pastries hits me. It's 4.20 in the afternoon, Athens time, we're two hours ahead of London. I haven't eaten since early this morning, I only had time for a small slice of toast and I'm starving.

I quickly pop into the baker's shop to buy a *tyropita* (cheese pie) and a take-away coffee, then look around for a cab.

Almost instantly a yellow cab pulls up beside me - Greek bouzouki music blares from inside.

'Mont Parnes Teleferique?' I ask, poking my head through the open window.

The driver nods, I open the back door and slide inside.

Athens is always busy and today's no exception, it should only take about twenty minutes to get to the teleferique, from there I'll take the cable car to the casino.

I sit enjoying the familiar sounds of Athens happy to be back. The sun's shining, it's a lovely day, I lean back and smile to myself.

The driver looks at me through his mirror. 'Your first time in Athens?"

'No, I used to live here.'

He nods and hums along to the song on the radio, it's one of my favourites.

I'm enjoying the ride so much I decide to keep the cab for the rest of the journey, this way I avoid the cable car which I'm not too keen on anyway.

A popular Greek song suddenly blasts from the car radio, the driver sings along, worry beads swing above the car dashboard, I smile to myself, I'm really enjoying this. Taking the cable car would've been quicker but I prefer driving through the familiar streets of Athens, there's so much to see.

After the divorce, my son and I returned to the UK and stayed with Mum for a while in Oxford. To say the experience was traumatic, not staying with Mum, but the horrific events which occurred, is an understatement. When we eventually moved to London, I rented an apartment, found a school for Jamie and got a job. We've been there ever since. My ex lives here in Athens.

The cab climbs higher and higher, up the narrow mountain road, small icons in memory of those who've lost their lives are on many of the corners. The roads are quite treacherous, you really need to be a good driver if you're driving here.

When I was a teenager, I was in one of the old buses

going to Mont Parnes, we were half-way up and the bus suddenly stopped and began sliding backwards. We were just a few inches from the edge. I can still remember the screams and shouts of sheer panic, the bus driver shouting, '*grígora, grígora érchontai sto brostinó méros tou leoforeíou*,' (quickly, quickly, come to the front of the bus). The weight of everyone moving forward saved us from going over.

Just thinking about it reminds me of the dizzying drop below us. We drive higher and higher up the mountain until at last the cab stops outside the casino.

After paying the driver, I stand inhaling the crisp mountain air and familiar scent of pines. I used to love coming here, I wonder what it's like now.

I walk up the steps, go through the doors and see Helen waiting for me.

She runs over and hugs me. 'Let's go to the restaurant, it's not very busy, I was there just now having coffee with the French guys.'

Then she holds me at arm's length and gives me a knowing look. 'How was the journey? I noticed you came by cab, still worried about the cable car?'

I make a face.

Helen laughs. 'Come on, let's get something to eat.'

As soon as we enter the restaurant a waiter hurries over to meet us.

'A table for two by the window, if you have one,' Helen says, grabbing my arm.

He nods. 'Follow me.'

He leads us to a table with a view overlooking Athens. I order a *salade niçoises*, without the fish, and wait for Helen to order.

'Helen,' I murmur, giving her a nudge. 'Do you want to order?'

'Oh, sorry, I'll have the same as you, Beth.'

I can't believe it. Helen isn't vegetarian, she loves fish.

'Are you sure? You want the *salade niçoises*, without fish?'

'Yes, that's fine.'

'Okay, two s*alade niçoises*, without fish, some olive bread and a bottle of sparkling water.'

The waiter nods and leaves. I break off a piece of crusty looking roll from a basket on the table and look closely at Helen, she looks worried and pale.

'So how was the meeting, with the French guys?'

'Oh, it went well, in fact it was good, I may be going to Nice to finalize things next month, they want me to meet their other partner.'

'That's fantastic! We should celebrate, I'll order some champagne?'

'No, not now, we can celebrate tonight.'

She sits flicking through her phone then stares out of the window a worried look on her face.

I lean forward and grab her hand. 'What's wrong, Helen?'

She takes a deep breath, then looks at me. 'It's James, we arranged to meet last night, then he called and said he had to meet someone about a story. He didn't say much, just that he was going to a bar in Glyfada.'

She stops and frowns. 'He said he'd be a little late, but he didn't turn up. I tried calling him, but it just went to voicemail. I just called his home number and his wife answered.' She hesitates for a second, then asks. 'Did you know he's married?'

I shake my head. 'No, I didn't know. What did his wife say?'

'She didn't know where he was.'

'Try not to worry Helen, maybe he met someone, had a little too much to drink, booked into a hotel...'

Just then the waiter arrives with our food, fills our glasses with sparkling water and leaves us to it.

Helen doesn't touch her food but I'm hungry, the salad is delicious, the olive bread divine. After a bit of encouragement on my part, she eats a little then stops.

'You know, the economic crisis has had a devastating effect on many people in Athens. James's delicatessen hasn't been doing well but my travel agency still makes a profit.'

'That's great, shame about James though.'

'He has a share in the business, don't you remember? I borrowed some money from him when things were tough. I think his wife's jealous. She wants him to sell his share.'

'But doesn't she know you're married? Surely she knows you've been friends since you were children?'

'Yes, of course she does.' She sits nervously twisting a serviette. 'I've tried being nice to her, but she's always so nasty.'

I top up our glasses with sparkling water and hand Helen hers. 'Here, drink this and don't worry so much. Maybe his wife knows who he was meeting, did you ask her?'

'When I asked if she knew where he was, she just said no and put the phone down.' She gives me a sad look. 'James said things aren't so good at home, they rarely speak, it's a bit like me and Theo.'

Now I am surprised. 'What's happened with you and Theo?'

She shrugs and looks away.

She obviously doesn't want to talk about it now, so I ask her about James. 'Have you any idea which bar he would go to?'

'I don't know, all he said was that it was a bar near the beach.' She fidgets with her serviette and frowns. 'You know what James is like, if he was going to be late, he'd phone, he wouldn't leave me waiting like that, especially late at night.'

I've finished eating, Helen's hardly touched hers. I can tell she's worried so suggest we go back to Athens; we can talk about it on the way down. We pay the bill then walk over to the teleferique.

The cable car arrives, we pile in with the others, I hold my breath, I don't look out of the window. Helen says nothing, just stares ahead, miles away. It doesn't take long, it's much quicker than driving.

Seven minutes later we're down, we take the waiting bus to Syntagma Square. Helen sits looking out of the window, I check my phone.

'You can't imagine how awful it's been, Beth,' she suddenly blurts out.

'What do you mean?' I ask, watching her closely. 'Work or Theo?'

She laughs. 'I wish it was work. It's Theo, he picks on the slightest thing I do to make me feel bad, he even said I should go to night school, to improve my Greek.'

'But your Greek is good. He's the one who needs lessons.' I could say more but stop.

She nods and shrugs. 'It got so bad I didn't want to go home, I threw myself into my business, it's the only place I feel I'm in control.'

Now I know why she works so hard. Poor Helen, I wish she'd told me.

She sits fidgeting with her phone, then looks at me. 'He's not the same Beth, he's changed so much, I hardly recognize him.'

Now you're seeing the real man you married, I want to

say, but don't. I always had a bad feeling this would happen. Even though Greece is in financial meltdown, her husband still makes a lot of money from his nightclub. The tourists keep coming and there are always wealthy Greeks with money to spend.

'But why don't you leave him?'

She looks at me in surprise. 'It's not as easy as that, you should know, Beth.'

She's right, I'm the last person to give advice. When I discovered how many years my ex had lied to me about money and other things I asked for a divorce. I still don't know if he was involved in that terrible case in Athens, I also never found out if he was having an affair, but deep down I know he's guilty of both.

She looks at me for a long minute, then shrugs. 'I can't believe that this is happening to me, Beth. One day I found a ring in my bed, another time I received a phone call from a girl saying my husband loves her and that I should move out, let them be together. She said he's going to divorce me and marry her.'

I can hardly believe what I'm hearing, this isn't the Helen I know, why is she still living with him? I lean forward so nobody can hear me. 'Why do you take it? Kick him out!'

Helen bites her lip. 'He's lied so much, and I'm so stupid I believed him. He said the ring was probably mine and that I'd forgotten I had it.'

I'm amazed but not surprised. 'Why didn't you phone me or come to London? You know you can always stay with me.'

'I didn't want to worry you. James is here, I used to talk to him about it.'

'What did he suggest you do?'

'He gave me the number of a friend he knows from

London, he said he might be able to help, he studied law but I'm not sure what he does now.'

'So, did you contact him?'

'Yes, he's having Theo followed to find out what he's up to. This morning he showed me some photos and a video.'

I raise my eyebrows. 'Were they of Theo?'

She nods, for the first time I see hatred in her eyes. 'Yes, he was with various women, he was having sex with them.' She sits staring into space. 'I have no idea how he got them, but he did...'

She turns and looks at me. 'I'm getting a divorce, Beth.'

'Good, I'm going back to London in a few days you can stay with me and sort yourself out.'

'I can't, I've arranged to see a lawyer about the divorce and now I'm worried about James.'

Now I'm also getting worried, I know someone needs to be missing for a certain amount of time before the police will investigate, but I've no idea how it works in Greece. 'Okay, for now we must concentrate on James. Do you know any of his friends?'

'Only Kostas, I met him a few times with James. He gave me a card for his shop in Monesteraki. I called him last night, but he doesn't know where James is, he said he'd ask a few friends. I arranged to see him early this evening, do you want to come with me?'

'Oh Helen, I can't, I promised I'd deliver a birthday present for a friend in London, it's for her mother she lives near my hotel, it's her birthday today. Why don't you go and see Kostas, then we can meet up for dinner, I'm staying at the Plaka Hotel.'

The bus turns into Syntagma Square, then abruptly stops. Helen walks with me to my hotel then goes to meet Kostas.

5

HELEN & KOSTAS

ATHENS
5 February

AS I DRAW near the small Byzantine church of Agios Eleftherios, I hesitate for a minute and stand staring at it. Inside is an icon which is said to perform miracles, I never thought about it much until today, I can't resist and go inside.

After a few minutes I tear myself away from the tiny church and carry on walking down Ermou Street which as usual is a hive of activity. It leads to Monesteraki Square which as well as being a popular tourist hotspot is a hub for young people. They sit around playing guitars or just sit smoking and often break out into dance. The tourists seem to love the atmosphere, they also enjoy searching the shops for souvenirs to take home to their loved ones.

Kostas said his shop was located near the restored Turkish Mosque which is now a ceramics museum, he said that its opposite the metro. I search for a couple of minutes then suddenly I'm right outside his shop, the door is open, I knock and go inside.

From behind a curtain a Greek girl with short spiky purple hair suddenly appears. 'Yes, can I help you?' she asks.

'Is Kostas here?'

She nods and a few minutes later Kostas appears from behind the curtain. As soon as he sees me, he rushes over to me. 'Any news?' he asks, frowning.

I shake my head. 'I was hoping you had some.'

'I've phoned everyone I can think of,' he mutters. He stops and gives me a worried look. 'He hasn't been seen since yesterday afternoon.'

'What about the delicatessen?'

He shakes his head.

'Someone must have seen him,' I snap, feeling the despair rising inside me.

He says nothing just looks worried.

'Did you ask his wife?'

He runs his hands through his thick black hair. 'I tried phoning her, but there's no reply.'

'It doesn't make sense; someone must have seen him.'

'But I've tried everywhere I can think of, I'm sorry.'

Whilst he's talking, I scribble my number on a piece of paper and hand it to him. 'If you find out anything, anything at all, please call me?'

He takes the paper and mumbles something. I nod and leave the shop feeling even more worried. I know they often have a drink together and if Kostas can't find him, who can?

Maybe I should call the police, but what about his wife?

6

BETH

Athens, 5 February
Plaka Hotel

I'm nearing the hotel when my phone rings, it's Helen.

'Beth, I'm nearly at your hotel, where are you?'

'I'm just going inside, come to the top floor, I'll be on the terrace.' As I go inside the receptionist beckons me over and hands me an envelope.

'It's a message for you.'

I'm surprised, not many people know I'm in Athens. I called work to let them know I'd arrived, and I've also spoken to Mum. I quickly scan the contents of the small envelope. It's from my ex, he wants to see me, how strange, how does he know I'm here?

I take the lift to the terrace, there's an empty table with a good view of Athens, I hurry over and sit down.

The waiter comes over. 'A cold beer, please.'

He nods and returns to the bar.

There's a newspaper laying on the table in front of me so I pick it up and glance at the headlines...

SHOOTING IN ATHENS BEACH BAR LATE THIS EVENING - ONE DEAD - ONE IN A COMA.

I sit staring at it for a few minutes. Didn't Helen say James was meeting someone in Glyfada?

The waiter brings me my beer, I mutter my thanks whilst staring at the newspaper, it's just a coincidence, it must be.

I'm still sitting staring at the newspaper when Helen arrives.

'I just saw Kostas,' she murmurs, sitting down and giving me a worried look. 'He checked around and nobody's seen James since yesterday afternoon. I'm getting worried Beth, maybe we should call the police?'

Then she notices the newspaper in front of me and sees the headline. A look of horror appears on her face. 'James, it could be James.'

'I know, that's what I was thinking.'

She suddenly jumps up. 'We must go to the hospital. We must see if it's James.'

I quickly scan the article again. 'It doesn't mention the name of the hospital, is there one in Glyfada?'

Helen's face is as white as a sheet. 'I don't know,' she mutters. 'Will the police know?'

I'm pacing around the terrace, oblivious to the stares from nearby tables. I look at the newspaper again and groan. 'We need to speak to the journalist who wrote it.'

A few minutes later I'm calling the newspaper and ask to

speak to Elias Demetriades, the journalist who wrote the article. I'm told he's not there, but I can leave a message. I say it's urgent, it's about the shooting at the bar in Glyfada and that we think it might be our friend. I leave my name and phone number and we wait.

Ten minutes later my phone rings.

'Hello, I have a message to call you.'

Helen comes close so she can hear what he's saying.

'Yes, that's right,' I reply. I hold my phone close to Helen. 'It's about the shooting in Glyfada last night.'

'You think it might be your friend? Is this correct?'

Yes, we need to know the names of the people involved, or the address of the hospital.'

There's a short pause, so I close my eyes, willing him to tell me.

'You must understand, this is being handled by the police, I can't give out any names.'

'Yes, I understand but we need to know if it's our friend. I'm staying at the Plaka Hotel, near Syntagma Square. The owner knows me, he can vouch for me. I'm a freelance journalist - I'm here to write an article on the political situation in Greece. My friend lives here, she's married to a Greek. Please can you tell me something?'

'Where are you now?' he asks.

'We're on the terrace of the Plaka Hotel.'

He hesitates for a few seconds. 'Okay, I'll be there in about ten or fifteen minutes.'

'*Signome* (excuse me), are you Beth Papadakis?'

I nod and gesture for him to sit down.

He looks tired, he has black hair speckled with gray, he's probably in his 40s or 50s and stockily built.

'Yes, I'm Beth, this is my friend Helen, I have my passport...'

'No, don't worry,' he says, shaking his head, 'I saw the manager downstairs.'

He pulls out a chair and sits down, lights a cigarette, then quickly blows the smoke away from us. 'I'm sorry, I forgot we can't smoke here anymore.' He stubs it out, then turns and looks at us.

'You want to know if your friend is one of the men in the bar, don't you?'

We look at him and nod.

'Two men were involved, one Greek the other English.'

Helen gasps. We both sit very still and wait.

He looks at us with sad eyes. 'The English man is on a life support machine. What is the name of your friend?'

Helen looks at me, then at him. 'James, his name is James, James Baldwin.'

He sits staring at us, then shakes his head. 'Yes, it's him.'

Helen bursts into tears.

He leans forward and gently murmurs. 'He is also my friend, we worked together.'

Tears stream down Helen's face as she looks at him. 'I want to see him. Can you take us to him?'

'Of course, my car is outside.'

We pile into his old blue Renault convertible which is parked outside the hotel, me in the front with him, Helen in the back. We drive along in silence passing brightly lit shop windows and graffiti covered buildings, a stark reminder of the present political situation in Athens. On the way Elias calls the hospital to let them know we're coming.

After about twenty minutes we arrive at the hospital. It's strangely quiet. Elias speaks to a nurse, then we're led to a room, she opens the curtains surrounding the bed and we gasp.

James's head is covered with bandages, half his face is visible, a small piece of his red hair is poking out from the bandage. His eyes are closed, he's hooked up to a machine.

I stand transfixed, staring at him. Helen rushes over and holds his hand.

'I must talk to the nurse,' Elias says. 'I'll be back in a minute.'

After a few minutes Elias returns and beckons for us to follow him outside. 'The next few hours are crucial for James,' he murmurs as we walk to the waiting room. 'The nurse said for us to wait outside, sit here and I'll get some coffee.'

As soon as he's gone Helen grabs my arm. 'I'm not staying here; I'm going to see James.'

A few minutes later Elias returns with three coffees, he hands me one and places one on a chair for Helen. Dark shadows and lines are etched under his eyes, he looks exhausted.

'Elias, you must be tired. Why don't you go home?'

He doesn't reply, just sits looking at his coffee.

'Elias, it's good of you to bring us here, but we can get a cab back to the hotel.'

He shrugs. 'But he's my friend, I want to be here. Why don't you get some sleep? You've been travelling all day, if anything changes, I will call you.' He looks around. 'Where is Helen?'

Just then the nurse comes over and whispers something in Elias's ear.

Oh no! Please, let James be alright!

He looks over and sees the look on my face. 'No, the nurse said he's stable for the moment, but you should get some sleep. Go back to the hotel, I'll call you if there's any change.'

I know he's right, but will Helen agree?

I go to the ward and gently draw back the curtain. Helen's talking quietly to James, I bend over and whisper. 'The nurse says it's best if we get some sleep, we need to be strong. They have our number. If there's any change, Elias will call us.'

She nods, whispers something to James, and then follows me to the waiting room.

'I'm staying at your hotel tonight, Beth, I'll check to see if they have a room near you.'

On the way back she calls the hotel and the room next to mine is available, it has intercommunicating doors.

Elias drops us off, then drives back to the hospital, Helen collects her key and we go to our rooms.

With the intercommunicating doors open it's like one huge room. We take off our coats and crawl into bed, I'm sure I won't sleep but eventually I nod off.

7

BETH

Athens - Plaka Hotel

Early morning - 6.05 am

My phone's ringing, for a minute I don't know where I am, then I remember. James, the hospital, my heart sinks.

Helen's sitting up in bed, a dazed look on her face.

'Hello,' I mumble into the phone while crawling out of bed.

'This is Elias. You must come quickly.'

Helen sees the look on my face and leaps out of bed. We grab our bags and run downstairs to reception.

Within minutes, we're in the back seat of a cab on our way to the hospital, Helen's cursing herself for not staying with James. It feels as if everything's running in slow motion, this isn't happening, but I know it is. The streets are empty, it's early in the morning, I sit grimly staring out of the window.

When we arrive, we leap from the cab and run inside. My heart skips a beat, Elias is standing there with tears streaming down his face.

Helen grabs hold of me. 'No! Not James!'

This is the moment we've been dreading. We're too late. We run past Elias to the room where James is. Helen lets out a moan when she sees him. I can't breathe, tears stream down my face. The nurse comes in and asks us to go with her. After kissing James, we follow her to another room where Elias sits with his head in his hands. The nurse sits beside him, she speaks in Greek, she says she must call James's wife, to let her know what's happened.

He nods and looks over at us. 'Come, I'll take you back to your hotel.'

Just a few hours ago we thought James would make it, that he would pull through, that he would be okay, none of us thought this would happen. We sit in silence as Elias drives us back.

As we pull up outside the hotel Elias turns and looks at us. 'I now have to write a news flash...' He hesitates then goes on. 'It will be in the morning paper and on TV.' He wipes a tear from his face and mutters. 'If I can do anything to help, please call me.'

He hands me his card. I nod and take it. We silently get out of the car, he drives off.

Helen stands shaking her head. I gently pull her inside the hotel.

'Let's go to the café, I can't face going to our room, can you?'

She nods.

The café's empty, we sit in a corner away from the other tables, Helen buries her head in her hands, I hold onto her.

Nothing can take away the dreadful pain and emptiness we feel.

Suddenly a waiter appears, he knows what's happened, he was the one who called the cab for us to go to the hospital. He murmurs his condolences and places two glasses of brandy on the table, then leaves.

'I can't believe he's gone, it's like a terrible nightmare,' Helen sobs. 'Why would anyone kill James?'

We sit like this for well over an hour, drinking brandy and talking about James, trying to work out what happened.

Helen gets up, then curls up on a nearby sofa, her pale, tear-stained face is hidden by her long brown hair.

A few hotel guests come in and peer at us, probably wondering what's wrong.

I shake her gently. 'Let's go upstairs, have a lay down, we need to sleep.'

'I can't,' she mumbles. 'I have an appointment with a lawyer, about my divorce and I...' Tears well up in her eyes, she covers her face with her hands. 'Oh Beth, it's so horrible, who would do such a terrible thing.'

I don't say anything, if I do, I know I'll start crying, so I just shake my head.

'I have to call James's wife, I must offer her my condolences.' Her voice brakes, she shudders, then draws in a deep breath. 'I must find out when the funeral is.'

She gives me a hug, then leaves.

I make my way to the terrace, it's better to be with people, not talking to them but having them around me. The thought of going to my room fills me with dread. The sound of pots and pans from the hotel kitchen all sound so normal, its breakfast time - but nothing is normal, James is dead and nothing can bring him back.

I find a quiet corner away from it all and call Elias. It rings a few times then goes to voicemail. I leave a message to come to the hotel, around seven this evening, if he can. I sit holding my phone, staring ahead. The terrace is filling up with tourists planning their day ahead, they all look so happy.

I look over towards the Acropolis, the sacred rock, and in a strange way this makes me feel better, I always get a sense of peace when I'm near the ancient monuments of Greece. They've stood the test of time and witnessed more than their share of sadness, it's early, so if I go now, I'll have the place to myself.

The tiny streets of Plaka wind upwards, towards the Acropolis, I follow where they lead, past spotlessly clean blue and white houses with windows open, cats laying stretched out, basking in the morning sun, some are on windowsills, others lay curled up in flowerpots. Bougainvillea tumbles over them as if sheltering them while they sleep.

I don't go to the main entrance of the Acropolis, I'm taking the old route to the sacred rock it makes me feel closer to the real Athens. The higher up I go, the steeper the climb and the hotter I get, I feel exhausted and sit on a small white wall with the Parthenon towering above me.

I sit like this for a long time, thinking of James. The February sun warms me, but it can't take away my pain. Suddenly my throat feels dry. I need a drink.

THE HUM and buzz of waiters preparing for the day ahead, feels somehow comforting as I slowly walk down the tiny streets, past restaurants perched along the rocks. Strains of soft Greek music, the rustle of tablecloths being laid over small tables soothes my nerves. It's not as empty as before, it's still peaceful, but it won't be for long. I decide to find a place to sit and have a drink.

A little café catches my eye. It's not very busy so I find a corner table and order a fresh lemon juice.

When the waiter's gone I sit looking at the Parthenon. The secret tunnels around and under the Acropolis have always intrigued me, maybe now's a good time to find out exactly where they are. It will give me something to do, I must keep myself busy, stop thinking.

I sit hunched over my phone searching Google for information on the secret tunnels of Athens. There's not as much as I thought there would be, but then I find a video. I'm just about to watch it when a shadow falls over me.

'Do you mind if I sit here?' a man asks, pointing to the chair next to me.

I wave my hand to the chair opposite, but he sits next to me. I glance around at the empty tables then directly at him, but he just ignores me and calls the waiter over.

He orders a coffee then turns to me. 'Are you here on holiday?'

I'm not in the mood to have a polite conversation with anyone so I just nod and start getting ready to leave.

He leans back in his chair and looks intently at me. 'You don't remember me, do you?'

I have no idea who he is and suddenly feel very tired. 'I think you've made a mistake,' I mumble, searching for a few coins to pay for the drink. I push back my chair and go in search of a cab.

There's one coming down the street, I frantically wave it down.

'Plaka Hotel,' I mutter, clambering inside the cab.

For some reason I turn and look out of the back window.

The man who sat next to me - he's walking behind the cab - he looks up and smiles at me - it's a nasty, weird smile.

With a screech of tires, the cab speeds away.

8

HELEN

Athens - Kolonaki Square

Next day

The walk from the Plaka hotel did me good, but as I approach my house, I start thinking of James. He knew I was near. I felt his fingers tighten ever so slightly in my hand, but at the end I wasn't with him, he was all alone. I'll never forgive myself for not being with him.

I'm just about to open the door when I remember the other morning. Will Theo be here? His car isn't outside, so I quietly open the door, tiptoe inside, and stand listening in the hallway, nobody's here.

After a quick shower, I dress, get ready to leave, then go onto the balcony to see if Theo's car is here, thankfully it's not. The scent of jasmine from the flowers makes me think of James. He was so full of life and a wonderful friend, what a waste, what a terrible waste.

Biting down hard on my lip, I grab my bag and run downstairs. I'm just about to leave, when I think of the funeral. In Greece things move quickly. Then I remember Elias said he had to write a newsflash.

I run into the living room and switch on the TV. The news is on. A doctor is talking to a reporter about James, I feel dizzy so sit down, I need water.

I get up and run to the kitchen, gulp down a glass of water, then try to think. I don't want to talk to James's wife, but we need to know about the funeral. I take out my phone, tap in her number and wait. On the second ring she answers.

'Isabelle, this is Helen, I just wanted to say how sorry I am, I...'

The phone goes dead, she's hung up.

Then it suddenly rings. It must be her. She didn't mean to hang up.

But it's not his wife its Kostas. He's in a terrible state. He's just seen the news about James on TV. We talk for a while then I ask him if he can speak to James's wife as she won't speak to me, he says no.

'But Kosta, you must, she won't speak to me. Maybe she's in shock. I know things move quickly in Greece, and we must find out about the funeral.'

He sounds near to tears. 'I'll try, but I wasn't very close to his wife, she may not talk to me.'

'Kosta, you must try, we need to know when the funeral is.' I hear a muffled okay, and then call Beth.

'I just called James's wife, she won't speak to me, I can't believe it - she put the phone down.'

'Maybe she's in shock. How long has he been married?'

'A couple of years, he married her on the spur of the moment. Oh no, I've just remembered, James said she's pregnant.'

'Listen Helen, we need to know about the funeral, call her again or shall I try?'

I take a deep breath to stop my voice from shaking. 'He was like a brother to me Beth, I can't bear it...'

'Helen, try not to think about it, shall I come over?'

'No, I'm going to see my lawyer, I also have to see James's friend, the one who's helping me.' She stops and takes a couple of deep breaths. 'I must talk to him he needs to know what's happened.'

'Okay, we'll talk about it later. By the way, I've been thinking, you said he's a friend of James so surely he can help us find out who did this? Can you arrange for us to meet, maybe tomorrow, at the hotel? Oh, and what's his name?'

'I'll try and arrange something, his name is Dev. Now I really must go, Beth. I'll see you later at the hotel.'

I lock the door and leave the house, there's a squeal of tires, a car races towards me, I jump back into a small recess of the doorway and the car just misses me.

Then it starts reversing back.

'What the hell are you doing?' shouts a voice from above me.

I look up. It's my next door neighbour. He's hanging over his balcony, waving his fist at the driver. It seems to work because the next minute, with a squeal of tires, the maniac drives off and disappears down the street.

My neighbour curses, then peers down at me. 'Are you okay?'

'Yes,' I reply, stepping out onto the pavement and

looking up at him. 'Thank you so much, if it hadn't been for you...'

'Glad I could be of help; I only wish I had time to take his registration number down. If I were you, I'd be very, very careful, that was no accident, he did that deliberately.'

'I will, and thanks again.'

He shakes his head, 'No problem.' Then he points to a cab coming down the street. 'If I were you, I'd get in that cab, before that maniac comes back.'

9

BETH, HELEN & ELIAS

ATHENS - PLAKA HOTEL
Later that evening

AFTER A QUICK SHOWER, I dress, then make my way to the terrace. I order an ice-cold beer and sit looking around me. It's strange, but even though Athens has been going through the worse crisis since the Second World War, the tourists keep coming.

A table at the edge of the terrace suddenly becomes free, so I quickly move tables and peer down at the street below. I can see Helen and Elias, they've just spotted each other.

A few minutes later they're on the terrace.

'How are you, Beth?' Elias asks, trying his best to smile. He looks tired, his face is drawn and there are dark circles under his eyes. 'Did you manage to get some sleep?'

I shrug. 'No, I didn't sleep. I went to the Acropolis then I had a drink.'

He looks at us sadly and nods. 'Yes, it's best to keep busy. I spent the day covering another protest against the government's reform plans.' He stops and looks around the terrace. 'Shall we eat here or find somewhere else?'

I shrug my shoulders. 'I really don't mind where we eat, I'm not very hungry.'

Raising his eyebrows, he nods and sighs. 'You must try to eat something, Beth, keep your strength up.'

I'm just about to say something, but he carries on…

'There's a very good restaurant in the Psiri district of Athens, it's not far from here. Shall we try it?'

'I'm not hungry, but if everyone is going, I'll come,' Helen says, looking at me.

I nod and pull on my thick cardigan. 'Good idea Elias, a walk will do us good.'

It's February and the streets are full of tourists; it feels more like summer than the end of winter. We walk along in silence. Helen looks sad and tired, I link my arm through hers and give her a hug.

'So, what did the lawyer say?'

She shrugs, then suddenly stops and looks at me. 'Something awful happened today, before I met the lawyer.'

I stop dead in my tracks, imagining the worse. 'What, another row with Theo?'

'No, it wasn't him, he wasn't there.' She looks at Elias, then at me, as if wondering whether to tell us or not.

'So, what happened?' I ask, watching her closely.

'It was really scary, I'd just opened the door and was leaving the house, a car appeared from nowhere, it came straight at me. I had to jump back into the doorway, I was lucky it just missed me, otherwise ...'

'Why didn't you call me?' I splutter, staring at her in amazement.

'I didn't have time, Beth, it was so awful, the guy started reversing back into me. Thankfully my neighbour was on his balcony. He shouted at him, so the guy stopped and drove away. If he hadn't been there...'

Elias and I look at each other. He takes out his phone and walks a few yards ahead of us.

'Did you get his registration number?' I ask, thinking at least then we'd have something to go on.

'No, it happened so fast.'

Elias shoves his phone back in his jacket and walks back to us. 'I just called my friend Dev, he said try not to go anywhere alone, at least not until we find out who did this.'

Helen looks at him in surprise. 'Dev, Dev Salter?'

He nods. 'I met him through our mutual friend, James.'

At the mention of James's name, we all seem to freeze. I'm thinking maybe we shouldn't be walking along the streets of Plaka like this, what if this maniac is following Helen?

I look over at Elias, he's deep in thought. 'Look, we can't just walk along like this as if nothing's happened.' I stop walking and look at them both. 'We're in a traffic free zone now, but it will soon change, so to be on the safe side, maybe we should get a cab?'

Helen looks surprised. 'Why should we? I want to walk.'

'Okay, but we must be careful. Anything's possible in these small streets, just keep your eyes and ears open.'

They both nod in agreement and we carry on walking, but at least now we're all keeping our eyes on the street ahead and listening for the sound of a car speeding towards us.

Ten minutes later, Elias stops outside a traditional

looking restaurant on Platia Iroon. 'This is the restaurant, it's one of the oldest in Psiri and one of the best, come on, let's go inside.'

At the back of the restaurant are trays of cooked food, left over from lunch. One tray contains giant broad beans cooked in a tomato sauce. Another contains lamb casserole with peas and potatoes. There are stuffed peppers and artichokes, sauté potatoes and pastichio – a type of macaroni cheese. Despite it looking like a buffet restaurant, this is the way many restaurants in Greece operate. The food usually tastes better as it's had time to rest and absorb all the flavours.

We decide what to eat, then sit outside on the terrace. A few minutes later the waiter brings us a bottle of house red and a basket of sliced crunchy Greek bread. After a few minutes, he returns with a tray full of food. *Kolokithea keftedes* (courgette fritters) for me and *paidakia* (lamb chops) for Elias and Helen. A huge plate of sizzling hot chips and a large bowl of Greek salad are placed in the centre of the table for us to share.

Red candles glow in empty brandy bottles on round tables covered with pristine white tablecloths. Greek music plays softly in the background, we begin to relax. Elias munches away on his lamb chop whilst gathering chips with his fork. I can't help but smile, Greeks always seem to enjoy their food, no matter what. I wonder if he has a wife and kids at home, for some reason I don't think so, but he doesn't look the bachelor type.

'Are you married?' I ask, hoping he won't mind me asking.

He glances over and smiles slightly. 'I was, but now I'm divorced, I live alone, in an apartment just off Vassilias Constantinos.'

Grabbing a serviette, I wipe my mouth quickly. 'But that's near to where I used to live on the corner of Messoghion.'

Elias looks surprised. 'How long did you live there?'

'While I was married, then I left and went back to the UK.'

Helen suddenly looks up. 'When I first came to Athens, we used to go to the Hilton Hotel and have drinks on the roof-top terrace, do you remember, Beth?'

'Yes, it has fantastic views of the Acropolis.' I sit deep in thought. Alex and I did have some good times at the beginning.

While we're chatting, Elias moves his chair slightly away from us and answers his phone.

The waiter suddenly appears with a tray containing three Greek coffees and three glasses of brandy, compliments of the house.

I look over at Elias. He seems to know the waiter well. He probably comes here a lot. I wonder how long he's been divorced. It's strange, but we all seem to be in the same boat, two of us are divorced, and Helen's desperately trying to get one. This brief respite from the horror of the past few hours puts us all in a reflective mood.

We walk silently back to the hotel. Elias drives home, Helen books in for another night, then we go upstairs to our rooms.

'Have you heard from Theo?' I ask, wondering if he's contacted her again.

She's laying on her bed, still fully dressed. 'No, and I don't want to, he's probably at home, screwing someone on my bed.'

She turns over, closes her eyes, and a few seconds later she's asleep.

10

BETH & HELEN
Athens, Plaka Hotel
Breakfast time

HELEN ARRIVES LATE for breakfast looking pale, I'm on my second cup of coffee. She goes over to the bar, gets a coffee then sits next to me. She didn't mention her visit to the lawyer last night, probably because Elias was there.

'How did it go with the lawyer yesterday?'

She shrugs.

'Does he think you'll win?'

She nods. 'Yes, he said I'm sure to win'. The thought of it seems to brighten her up. 'He said I have a very strong case, he's in the process of arranging a date for the hearing.'

'Great! What about Dev, did you see him?'

'Yes, he's going to help.'

'So, when are we meeting him?'

She laughs. 'You really are keen, aren't you? I thought the café in Syntagma Square would be a good place to meet, there are lots of tables outside so it will be easier to talk without being overheard, it's the one in front of the Hotel Grande Bretagne.'

I nod. 'Sounds good, what time will he be there?'

'Around 11ish, is that okay?'

I glance at my phone. 'I need some photos of the parliament building for my article for work, so if I leave now I can take them and be at the café by 11.00, do you want to come with me?'

'No, I've a few calls to make, I'll see you there.'

I start walking to the elevator.

'Shall we let Elias know we're meeting Dev?' Helen shouts.

'No, it's Sunday, let him have a lay-in.'

I head over to Syntagma Square to the Parliament building, I'll get a few shots of the Evzones changing guard outside parliament, then I'll make my way to the café to meet Dev.

When I arrive, the place is packed with tourists waiting for the official changing of the guard, it happens every Sunday at 11.00am. I haven't had anything to eat yet so if I go straight to the café, I can have a quick bite to eat before Dev arrives, I can take photos of this another time.

The café terrace is practically empty, just a couple having breakfast. I go inside and order, then sit outside watching the comings and goings of people in the square. Then it suddenly hits me - I have no idea what Dev looks like.

The waitress arrives with my croissant and black coffee. Five minutes later I've finished my coffee and I'm brushing crumbs off my face. I have five minutes before Dev arrives so close my eyes and sit enjoying the warmth of the sun on my face. I can hardly believe it, so much better than the rain and cold in London. I stretch out my legs and listen to the sound of the traffic, it's strangely soothing to feel so relaxed amongst so much activity.

'Beth?'

'Yes?'

I quickly sit up, there's a slim dark-haired man, with piercing blue eyes smiling at me. 'Sorry, I was miles away,' I mumble. 'You must be Dev?'

He nods and looks at my empty cup on the table. 'Would you like something - another pastry, a coffee?'

I can see him eyeing the crumbs on my black top and smile. 'I think I've had enough.'

He smiles, sits in the chair opposite me and calls the waitress over.

'An espresso and...'

He looks at me.

I shake my head. 'No, thanks.'

'You have a good Greek accent but you're English, aren't you?' I say, watching as he takes out a packet of cigarettes.

He offers me one – I shake my head.

'Yes, I've been living in Athens on and off for a couple of years, what about you?'

'I live in London, I'm half Greek - my father's Greek, my mother's English. My Greek's a bit rusty, but I survive.' Now this could be interesting, I wonder why he's in Greece and what his story is. For some reason he doesn't look married, maybe he changed careers? He looks young but could easily be in his 40s. He's good looking in a serious sort of way. Suddenly I realize he's watching me and look away.

The waitress arrives with his coffee, then Helen arrives looking pale and tired.

'Coffee?' Dev asks, giving her a worried look.

She nods and looks at the waitress. 'Yes, an espresso

please.' She sighs and looks from Dev to me. 'We can't find James's wife. Kostas has been trying to help but it's useless, she's not at the delicatessen, so we'll have to go to their house in Faliron.'

I can tell Helen's about to burst into tears. 'Don't worry, have your coffee then we'll all go looking for her.'

'What's wrong with that woman,' Helen mutters. 'We need to know when the funeral will be.'

Dev quickly drinks his coffee. 'I'll go to the delicatessen; you stay here with Beth. I'm surprised Isabelle hasn't contacted me; I was expecting a call from her this morning.' He looks at us sadly. 'We all want to be there for James, he's been a good friend to me, we were very close.'

He suddenly looks very angry and I sense a sort of toughness I hadn't noticed before.

Helen looks at me. 'What do you think, Beth?'

I shrug. 'Well, we must sort this out or it'll be too late.' I bite my lip, wishing I hadn't said that.

Helen's lower lip trembles, then her phone rings, it's Kostas.

'He's on his way,' she says, putting her phone in her pocket. 'He'll be outside the Grand Bretagne Hotel in a few minutes, he's driving an old black Ford.'

The waitress arrives with Helen's coffee. Dev pays the bill, then looks at me.

'Give me your phone number, Beth, I might need it.'

After keying my number into his phone, he walks quickly out of the square, and across the road to where Kostas is waiting.

Helen sits watching them drive away. 'I hope his wife is there, otherwise it's a twenty-minute drive to Faliron, and it's getting late.' She sits biting her lip then pulls out a packet of cigarettes and lights one. We stay like this waiting for news.

After an hour we return to the hotel, Helen goes straight onto the balcony I go to the loo.

Two seconds later, my phone rings.

'Answer it Helen, I'm just washing my hands, it's next to my bed.'

I rush out of the bathroom.

'It's Dev,' she mumbles, handing me my phone. 'They can't find her.'

'What's happening, Dev?' I ask, taking the phone.

'The delicatessen's closed and she's not at their place in Faliron.'

'So, what are you going to do?'

'I'm not sure, I'll try and find out where she is, I'll call as soon as I know something.'

I can tell by his voice he's worried, he knows how close Helen and James were.

'Okay, call me as soon as you can.'

Helen's sitting on her bed staring into space, a strange look on her face.

'Let's go onto the balcony, Helen, and get some fresh air.'

She doesn't budge, just sits staring out of the window.

I go outside and sit watching the passing traffic.

Where the hell is Isabelle? She can't have left the country.

Then it comes to me.

'Helen,' I shout, running back into the room. 'The hospital, we must phone the hospital, they'll know.'

A few seconds later the ward nurse answers.

'This is Beth Papadakis, I was there yesterday, with my friends Helen and Elias. Our friend James - James Baldwin, he passed away early yesterday morning, can you tell me when the funeral is?'

After a brief silence she answers. 'Dev Salter just called.

He asked me the same question. He said he's a friend of James, and Elias Demetriades.'

'And what did you tell him?' I ask, holding my breath.

'Mrs Baldwin arranged for her husband's body to be taken from the hospital this morning for burial near the coast where they live. I thought you knew?'

'No, nobody contacted us.'

The phone slips from my hand.

Helen's shaking her head, a look of horror on her face.

I call Dev, after a few rings he answers. 'Dev, I just called the hospital, do you know where the funeral is? Do we have time to get there?'

There's a short silence and I know we're too late.

'I found the cemetery.' His voice sounds husky, I can hardly hear him. 'I'm next to James's grave, nobody's here. The cemetery workers told me it happened very early this morning.'

Tears well up in my eyes, Helen starts crying.

'Where are you?'

'I'll give you the address.' He hesitates for a second, then adds. 'Bring some flowers, I'll be waiting for you outside the gates of the cemetery with Kostas.'

I key the address into my phone, then we go in search of the nearest florist. Helen buys a large bunch of dark red roses, then we jump into a cab.

Twenty minutes later, we're outside the cemetery gates, Dev and Kostas are waiting for us.

With tears streaming down our faces, we make our way to where James lays. We all write our names and messages on a card the florist gave us, then tie it to the flowers.

Helen silently lays the flowers on the grave. There's no headstone, just a wooden cross with James written on it in

Greek. This is common practice - the headstone will come later.

Kostas drops Dev outside the Grand Bretagne Hotel.

'I'll call you later,' Dev says, slamming the car door behind him. His lips are pressed tightly together, his eyes no longer blue, but a steely gray colour.

I watch him walk into the hotel, there's a hard lump in my chest which won't go away.

Kostas drops us off outside our hotel and promises to keep in touch.

As soon as we reach our rooms, Helen goes straight onto the balcony; she lights a cigarette and sits staring into space.

'My flight's tomorrow Helen, I wish I could stay longer, come back with me for a few days?'

She inhales deeply. 'No, I've a lot to do.' A cold calm seems to have taken hold of her. She blows out the smoke and looks over at me. 'I'm going to get her for this.'

11

BETH

ATHENS AIRPORT

Back to London

IT'S NEARLY 11.00 am in the morning, my flight leaves at 11.30, I'll have to go through soon.

I'm worried about Helen. She's been very quiet since yesterday, I said I would stay, but she wouldn't hear of it, she said I had to get back to work.

I get up and give her a last hug. 'I'll call you as soon as I land in London, and for God's sake be careful, promise me you won't go out on your own, and remember to call Dev or Elias, if you must go out.'

I hesitate for a second. 'Sorry Helen, I sound just like Nick.' I bite my lip, even saying his name makes me shiver. I often wonder if the police have caught him. It happened last year when I left Athens and went back to Oxford, I still have nightmares about it. They said he was last seen in Malaga boarding a ferry, but for all I know he could be here in Athens.

'Don't worry about me Beth, and stop thinking about Nick.' She looks at me intently, then gives me a hug. 'He's in Spain somewhere, or Morocco.' Then as an afterthought she adds. 'Have you heard from that detective who was on the case?'

I shake my head.

'When you get to London say hello to your Mum and Jamie for me, and cheer up, I'll be in London soon.'

I nod. 'I hate leaving you here alone, especially after...'

'I'm okay Beth, I'll be careful, I know what to do.'

She looks tense, there are deep shadows under her eyes. She's supposed to have quit smoking, but she's puffing away like a chimney now.

'But I'm worried Helen, maybe I should stay a few days more.'

'Get on the plane, Beth, you have a job and a son to look after.'

I head towards customs then stop. She said, 'I know what to do.' *What's she going to do?* I have a sudden sense of foreboding and turn around and start walking back to her.

She frowns and motions with her hand for me to get on the plane. I give her a final wave. She turns and hurries out of the airport, she seems in such a hurry, I wonder where she's off to?

I go through customs, locate my flight on the overhead board, go over to the gate and stand in the queue. I know the last few days have been traumatic, but what the heck did Helen mean when she said *I know what to do*?

With one last look at Athens I board the plane for the four hour flight to London.

. . .

As soon as the plane lands, I call Helen. No reply, it goes to voicemail.

With a sense of unease, I walk through customs, then out of the building. The icy cold rain lashes down on my face and a cold blast hits me, the days of sitting in the sun are now just a distant memory.

Wrapping my coat tightly around me, I cross the road then take the escalator down to the Piccadilly line for the train to Earls Court. From there I'll take the Circle Line to Bayswater station.

A sudden rumbling sound breaks into my thoughts, the doors of the Tube slide open.

For the next 30 minutes I try calling Helen, but it keeps going to voicemail.

At last the train comes screeching to a halt at Bayswater station, I'm nearly home.

The rain-soaked pavements glisten as I leave the station, it's 4.10 in the afternoon and already dark, the streetlights are on and everyone's rushing around trying to keep warm.

I run to my block which is just a few minutes away, then into the warmth of the foyer. I'm on the first floor but as the elevator is here, I jump inside.

My apartment feels cold and empty, there's no Jamie to welcome me as usual, he's staying at Mum's. I flick the lights on, turn on the TV to wake the place up, then go into to kitchen.

For the past few months it's been just me and my son Jamie, he's staying with Mum in Oxford for a few days. I'll give them a call in a minute, let them know I'm back, but first I must have something to eat.

I switch on the small TV in the kitchen and put on the

news channel, I don't really want to hear about the doom and gloom of the latest crisis, but I'm used to having it on in the background. Now what will it be - a cheese sandwich? I'm searching in the fridge for some cheese when my phone rings, it's in my bag in the living room.

As soon as I get there it stops, it's an Athens number. I don't recognize it so call it back - number engaged. I try calling Elias's number but that goes to voicemail also.

With a sense of unease, I return to the kitchen, make my sandwich and take it into the living room.

After a while, the pitter-patter of rain against the window makes me feel sleepy. I didn't sleep much last night. I curl up on the sofa, cover myself with a throw and close my eyes.

A few minutes later my phone rings, it's an Athens number, it's the same number that called previously.

'Is that Beth Papadakis?'

'Yes, who is this?'

'Dr Diamakis, I need to talk to you, it's urgent.' There's a short pause, then he carries on. 'There has been an accident, we found your name and telephone number in her bag.'

I freeze. 'Whose bag?'

'Helen Panikos.'

'Hello, are you still there? Mrs Papadakis?'

'Yes,' I gasp, trying to keep my voice steady. I had a feeling something terrible was going to happen, but not this.

'How is she?'

'She's in a critical condition. She went through the windscreen of her car, she's unconscious.'

'I'll be on the next plane to Athens. Which hospital is she in?'

'Central Hospital, ask for me at reception, if I'm not here, ask for Dr Vronikis.'

I need a ticket and fast so instead of going online I call the travel agency in Queensway. 'Judy, this is Beth. It's an emergency. Can you get me on the next flight to Athens?'

'Is everything alright,' she asks. 'I mean you just came back.'

'It's Helen. She's had an accident.'

I hear her sharp intake of breath, then the patter of keys on her laptop.

'I can get you on the 6.10 from Heathrow - it's just gone 4.30, can you make it? I'll email you the ticket.'

As if in a trance, I stumble across the living room into the hall, cram my small laptop back into my luggage, I haven't had time to take anything else out. Grabbing my coat from the hall stand I leave my apartment.

It's dark outside, the cold rain lashes my face, but I feel nothing.

A black taxi turns the corner, I wave him down, wrench open the door, throw in my luggage, and climb inside.

'Heathrow Airport - drive as fast as you can.' Slamming the door shut I sit with my head resting on the window.

The driver peers at me in his mirror.

'Don't worry love, I'll get you there in time.'

I sit silently cursing the traffic and watch as the rain lashes the window. She said - *I know what to do*, what did she mean? I sit trying to remember other things she said that didn't make sense at the time. I had a feeling something was wrong. I sit cursing myself and the traffic then suddenly stop. When we came back from the cemetery and were in the hotel room Helen said *I'm going to get her for this,* what the hell did she mean?

Soon the taxi comes screeching to a halt outside the airport. I thrust a handful of money through the window to the driver and run to departures.

'Wait, wait,' the driver calls.

The rain's lashing my face, I keep on running.

'Miss, your luggage,' he shouts.

I turn around, the driver's running towards me with my carry-on luggage in his hand. I go to thank him but he puts his hand up to stop me.

'You don't have to thank me, just slow down or you'll have an accident.' With that he turns on his heel and runs back to his taxi.

I run into departures, go through customs, then run to the gate. The plane's ready for take-off, I board and stow away my luggage in the overhead rack. A woman in the seat next to me starts talking about how she hates flying. I mumble something, get up and move to another seat, at the far end of the plane.

The next minute one of the cabin crew arrives with my luggage. 'You forgot this,' she says, stowing it away for me. 'Thanks,' I mumble. 'That's really nice of you.' She smiles then goes to take her seat for take-off.

I fasten my safety belt and sit thinking of Helen, I should never have left Athens, I should have stayed with her, I should have called work, told them what happened – the article could wait. Jame's death may have tipped her over the edge. My mind's racing. I desperately need to talk to Dev or Elias. Do they know what's happened? Does Theo, her husband know? Then I have a terrible thought. Did he have something to do with this? Helen's trying to get a divorce. Did he find out? Then I think of James. Does this have something to do with James's murder? My eyes keep closing, I need to think, but I can't keep them open.

'*Prosecki parakalo* (attention please), we are now landing in Athens, please make sure your safety belts are fastened. Cabin crew take your seats.'

It's just gone midnight in Athens, the plane lands and when it stops, I pull down my luggage. I run to the exit and wait impatiently for the door to open. Then I run down the steps, across the tarmac and into the airport.

At last I'm in a cab heading for the hospital, I try calling Dev and Elias, but there's no reply.

12

ELIAS

ATHENS

Late afternoon - 4.55pm

ELIAS JUMPS out of his car with the photographer hard on his heels. The police cordoning off the shooting has brought traffic to the small street to a standstill. Elias runs over to a paramedic wheeling a stretcher to a waiting ambulance.

'What happened,' Elias shouts.

'Move out of the way,' yells the paramedic. 'This is an emergency.'

Elias can't help but look down and gasps.

The paramedic looks at him. 'Do you know her?'

Elias stares at the blood-stained body. 'Yes, it's my friend Helen. What happened?'

'She went through the screen, no idea how it happened, but I have to get her to the hospital fast.'

The doors of the ambulance close leaving Elias standing staring after it.

He turns, runs back to his car, jumps inside and follows the ambulance. With one hand on the driving wheel, he grabs his phone and shoves it into a bracket on the dashboard, then calls Dev.

'First it was James, now Helen!' Dev shouts. 'What the hell's going on?'

'I don't know,' Elias mumbles. 'I couldn't believe my eyes when I saw her... Only a few days ago I was looking at James on a stretcher, now it's Helen…' His voice breaks.

Dev sits with his elbows on his desk, rubbing his forehead. *Was it an accident or did someone try to kill her?* 'I'm leaving now,' he mutters. 'I'll see you at the hospital.'

Grabbing his jacket, he leaves his apartment, his car is parked outside the entrance to where he lives. The streets are quiet, so it doesn't take long and parking is easy.

Leaping out of his car he runs into the hospital, goes to reception and asks to see Helen. After what seems ages, he's taken to the emergency room where Helen lays. Blood seeps through the bandages covering her head, her eyes are closed. In desperation he turns to the nurse. 'Can't you do something to help her?'

The nurse just stands patiently watching him.

Then in a much lower voice he adds. 'You can't leave her here like this. She went through the window of her car you must stop the bleeding.'

'We are doing the best we can,' replies the nurse, stiffly. 'We are already under pressure with many other accidents.'

She's used to this type of reaction, but what can she do? A shortage of staff always adds to the stress and makes her job that more difficult.

'I will pay,' Dev exclaims. 'I want her to see a doctor NOW!'

'There's no need,' she answers, patiently. 'The doctor is on his way to see her. Please go outside and sit down.'

Dev stands shaking his head.

The nurse walks towards the door and opens it. 'Please, we're doing all we can, so don't worry.'

Elias suddenly appears in the doorway looking stressed and disheveled, he stares at Helen, then at Dev.

'Come,' Dev says. 'I think they want us to wait outside.' With his arm on Elias's shoulder they start to leave the room. 'We'll be outside if you need us,' Dev says.

After what seems a long time the nurse appears and motions for them to follow her to a nearby room.

'The doctor said she was very lucky, she's still concussed, but she's out of danger.'

Dev grabs a leaflet from a nearby table and scribbles down his number. 'Can you call me as soon as she wakes.'

She takes it and nods.

'When shall we come back?' Elias asks, frowning.

'Whenever you like,' replies the nurse, turning and opening the door. She rushes off to another emergency, they return to reception.

'Let's have a coffee, there's a small café not far from here,' Elias mutters.

They walk out of the hospital, cross the road and start walking towards the café.

'This is so terrible,' Elias groans. 'I can't get my head around it. Do you think this has something to do with James's murder?'

Dev shrugs. 'We have to check all the CCTV footage near the accident, then we might have something to go on. I already have the footage of where she lives.'

'How did you get it?' Elias exclaims, sounding surprised.

'This is highly confidential, my friend,' Dev replies. Then in a low voice, adds. 'We've been following her husband for a few weeks, we have the area covered with CCTV.'

He stops and frowns. 'It doesn't make sense, she went to the airport this morning with Beth, came home, then a little later she left the house and drove off quickly. They didn't say if anyone was following her so I'll check when I get back. Her cell phone was smashed in the accident, but we can check her home phone as we have that tapped.'

'What about her husband? Is he here in Athens?'

'I would think so, we must get someone to contact him, let him know what's happened.'

Then as an afterthought he quickly adds. 'Have you spoken to Beth? Does she know what's happened?'

'I tried to call her, but it keeps going to voicemail. Do you have another number for her?'

'No, I just have her cell phone number.'

Elias stops outside the small café and turns to Dev. 'Get a seat and I'll get the coffees, do you want something to eat?'

'No just a black coffee.'

Dev walks over to a small table at the back of the room and sits flicking through his phone.

A few minutes later Elias returns with two coffees and a toasted cheese sandwich. He hasn't eaten all day and is starving.

After hurriedly drinking his coffee, Dev stands up. 'I'm going back to the hospital, come over when you finish, I'll call if there's any change.'

13

BETH

ATHENS CENTRAL HOSPITAL

As I JUMP out of the cab, I see Dev going inside the hospital.

'Dev! Wait for me,' I shout.

He turns and stares at me as if he's seen a ghost.

'Have you seen Helen?' I gasp, running up to him.

He looks tired and shakes his head. 'I saw her for a few minutes, she was unconscious, she's had a few stitches in her head.'

We walk together to the hospital reception area and ask for her doctor. After a few minutes he comes over to talk to us, accompanied by a nurse.

'You must be Beth,' he says, taking my hand and shaking it. 'I spoke with you on the phone. I am Dr Diamakis.'

'Yes, I'm Beth, I just arrived from London, how is Helen?'

'She's out of danger, but she's still unconscious, you can

see her, but not for too long, she needs all the rest she can get.'

We follow the nurse to the ward where Helen is. Her eyes are closed, a bandage covers her head. I sit in the chair next to the bed. 'I'm here,' I say, grasping her hand.

Dr Diamakis comes over and stands by the bed, watching me.

'Have you taken any x-rays?' Dev asks, not taking his eyes off of Helen.

'Yes, she was lucky, it could have been much worse, be patient, the body is a complex machine.'

After a couple of hours, there's still no change, she's still unconscious. I keep nodding off in the chair next to Helen, Dev's outside on his phone.

Suddenly I feel someone prodding me.

'You must sleep for a while.'

I open my eyes, it's the nurse.

At that moment Dev comes into the room, he comes over to me, then turns to the nurse.

'Don't worry, I'm taking her to her hotel.' Then he quickly adds, 'If there's any change, call me?'

I can't believe he's suggesting leaving her alone. 'But I can't leave her like this, it's the same as when we left James at the hospital, the nurse said get some rest and then...'

'It's not the same, Beth,' he replies, looking at me intently. 'Helen's life is not in danger, she's going to be alright, you need to sleep. I'll drop you off at your hotel, then I'll come back here. If there's any change, anything at all, I promise I'll come and get you.'

We drive in silence to the Plaka Hotel and park outside.

'I'll get that,' he says, leaning over and taking my case from the back seat.

He's right, I am tired. I walk over to reception to collect

my key, everyone seems to know what's happened, news travels fast. Even the owner looks more subdued than usual. He stands shaking his head.

'Such a terrible thing to happen, poor Helen.' He squeezes my hand and says he'll send me up a brandy.

Then Dev comes in, he says hello to the owner then puts my case down next to me. 'Call me as soon as you're awake, okay?'

I nod. 'Thanks again for the lift.'

He smiles and walks back to his car, I take the elevator to my room.

The intercommunicating door is now locked, the room feels smaller than the last time I was here with Helen. Tears well up in my eyes, I should never have left her. I sit on the bed then rest my head on the pillow, I feel so tired and cold. There's a knock at the door, it must be my brandy.

I down the brandy in two gulps, cover myself with the duvet and close my eyes.

DOORS ARE OPENING AND CLOSING, I can hear people talking, I open my eyes and the morning sun streams through the shutters. Propping myself up on my elbow I reach for my phone. What time is it? Then it all comes back to me. Helen!

It's 9.15, there's no message from Dev, so I call him.

After a few rings he answers.

'How's Helen?'

'She's still the same. I'll come and get you, be at reception in fifteen minutes.'

After glugging down some water from the fridge I fill the hotel kettle with water – I must have a coffee.

A minute later I'm on my balcony sipping a black coffee.

I still can't believe Helen's in hospital, it feels surreal, we were here chatting together just a few hours ago.

I start pacing around the balcony, thinking about Helen.

A car suddenly hoots in the street below, I look down, it's Dev.

A few minutes later, we're driving quickly through the streets of Athens back to the hospital, the same hospital James was in. Dev glances over at me, as if he knows what I'm thinking.

'Did you stay at the hospital all night?'

He nods.

I had a feeling he would. He's the kind of person who does what he says. For someone who's been up all night, he seems incredibly wide awake. I glance at him through half closed eyes wondering if he can help find James's killer. Then I think of Helen. This wasn't an accident. The other evening, when we were walking to the restaurant with Elias, she told us about the driver who tried to reverse into her, no way was this an accident.

'What are you thinking?' Dev asks, suddenly.

I turn in my seat and look at him. 'I think you know. This wasn't an accident, was it? She said someone tried to run her down in a car when she was leaving her house. Elias called you and told you about it, do you remember?'

He just grunts.

'Dev, it must be the same person, and this time they got lucky.'

He says nothing, just opens his window and waits for the traffic to move. If only I hadn't left Athens she wouldn't be here now. I feel Dev looking at me again.

'It's not your fault Beth,' he mutters. 'Even if you'd been here, she wouldn't stay inside, you of all people should know that.'

I know he's saying this to make me feel better, but in a way he's right. The last words she said to me were - *I know what to do*. What did she do? Something which made someone want to kill her? Then I think of her phone.

Did she call someone before it happened?

I look at Dev. 'We must find her phone, check her last calls.'

He nods. 'Don't worry. We're doing all we can to find out who did this.'

His face is grim as we walk into the hospital.

While I sit with Helen, he goes to find the doctor.

14

BETH & DEV

ATHENS CENTRAL HOSPITAL

AN HOUR PASSES THEN Dev appears. 'The doctor said she's doing well, we just have to be patient.' He stands looking at Helen for a few minutes, then turns to me. 'Beth, I have to meet someone, but if you like, I can take you to see Elias, he has the police reports on the accident.'

'But I can't leave her alone like this!'

He raises an eyebrow. 'You have nothing to worry about, Beth.'

I can't believe it, I look at him and frown.

He seems slightly irritated. 'We have guards outside the ward and entrances, she's quite safe, I promise you.'

A few minutes later Dev drops me off outside a brightly coloured café. As I open the door, Greek music plays in the background and there's a strong aroma of coffee and black cigarettes, but no sign of Elias.

The guy behind the counter looks up and gives me a questioning look.

'*Thelo ena kafe parakalo.*' (Coffee please.)

He nods and carries on serving.

I pull out a stool near the window and hoist myself up. I can see Elias hurrying towards me, he's talking on his phone and clutching a wad of papers. He catches me looking and walks a bit faster.

'Have you ordered?' he calls, coming into the café.

'Yes, but I just ordered one coffee, I didn't know...'

The guy behind the counter catches his eye, Elias mumbles something to him, then he comes over and sits on the stool next to me. He plonks his papers on the small tabletop, swivels around and looks at me.

'How is Helen?'

'She's still unconscious, but the doctor says she's doing well.'

He sighs with relief. 'That's good, let's hope she wakes up soon.'

The guy arrives with our coffees, Elias makes room for them. After he's gone, he starts flicking through his pile of papers.

'Are they the police reports?'

He nods, but says nothing, just carries on reading.

I sit sipping my coffee waiting for him to show them to me, but he doesn't.

'Can I see them?' I ask. 'Dev told me you would show them to me.' Well, he didn't but that's what he implied, and that's why I'm here.

'*Sigá, Sigá* (slowly, slowly),' he mutters, reading another page of notes, 'I'm checking them now.'

He shuffles through them again, stopping only to make a few notes, then sighing deeply he turns to me. 'Beth, what I'm about to say may come as a shock.'

I nod and sit waiting for him to tell me.

A few seconds pass, then he grabs all the papers and slides off of the stool. 'Not here, let's go outside.'

'But...'

It's no use he's already paying for the coffees.

I slide off my stool and follow him. He walks quickly - his legs are longer than mine, I run to keep up with him.

'Come on,' he calls over his shoulder. 'My car is parked further along the street.'

'Where are we going?'

He doesn't reply, just clicks his car fob and his car lights up.

I slide into the front seat next to him. 'And what have you found out?' I have a good idea, but I want him to tell me.

He stares ahead at the traffic then glances at me. 'It seems the brakes on her car were cut.' He puts his foot down on the gas and moves into the faster lane.

'Do you have any idea who did it?' I yell, hanging onto the seat as the car lurches forward.

He grunts and gives me a sideways look. 'At the moment the police don't know.'

'Where are we going?'

'We're going to meet Dev.'

'But he just dropped me off, he said he was going to see someone?'

He nods. 'Yes, I know. His people have some CCTV footage he went to look at.'

'What do you mean his people?'

He doesn't reply, he just turns the radio on.

'Elias, I asked you a question.'

He doesn't say anything, just takes a sharp left, drives off the main highway and parks in a tree-lined side street full of apartment blocks and shops.

'Come on Beth, we're here.'

He hauls himself out of the car, I follow. We're not far from the beach, I can feel the sea breeze, it's a bit chilly, I'm glad I wore my coat.

Elias leads me into a small, darkish bar. A few men sit in a corner playing tavli, and in the far corner is Dev looking at his phone.

'Fancy seeing you again,' I say, walking over to him.

He smiles slightly. 'Yes, I'll tell you about it in a minute.'

He calls the waiter over and looks at me. 'What would you like to drink? Beer or maybe a wine?'

'A beer would be great.'

While we're waiting for our drinks to arrive Dev gives us an update.

'As you probably already know, we've had Helen's husband under surveillance for some time now, consequently this also includes Helen.'

I frown slightly, he carries on talking.

'From the CCTV we have in the area we found the following: Helen often parks her car outside their house, but during the evening she usually parks in the underground car park in the square.'

'Who's we?' I ask.

He looks at me sharply. 'Have you any idea who would want to kill Helen? What about her husband, is he capable of it?'

My opinion of Theo is very low, he's a nasty piece of work, but would he kill Helen? I look up and catch Dev watching me. He probably knows Helen told me about Theo.

'Her husband is selfish, he's a womanizer and until recently she was in denial about it.'

Dev gives me a questioning look. 'And?'

'What I don't understand is, if he wants to screw around with other women, why doesn't he ask Helen for a divorce?'

Elias sighs. 'Maybe he still loves her, in a warped kind of way. Many marriages are like this. Many people close their eyes to things they don't want to know.'

I snort. 'But he's a control freak, he wants his bread buttered on both sides.'

Elias looks confused, Dev sighs.

I explain what I meant. 'Sorry Elias, it's an English expression, it means he wants to screw around with other women, and still have Helen.'

Elias raises an eyebrow. 'So, he has no reason to kill her?'

'I don't think so. Helen seems to think he makes a lot from his nightclub, so that rules money out.' Or, does it? I look at Dev. 'Have you checked his finances? Do you know how much money he has stashed away?'

'He gambles a lot,' Dev replies, watching me closely. 'Did you know about that?'

I shake my head. 'No, I didn't. Helen's not short of money, her business is doing well, she has property in the UK, so if he has financial difficulties...'

Dev looks at me thoughtfully. 'Yes, we're checking his finances, we should have the results soon.'

'Whose *we* Dev, the company you work for?'

He gives me a funny look and gets up. 'Now I've got to be somewhere Beth, so Elias will drop you off at your hotel, if that's okay, or do you want to go somewhere else?'

'No, that's great.'

Dev goes to pay for the drinks, Elias is on his phone

talking to his office, and I'm still wondering why they don't tell me who Dev works for, what's the big secret?

As we leave the bar Dev turns to Elias and me. 'Shall we all have dinner tonight at that restaurant you like in Psiri?'

Elias nods. 'It's good for me.'

Dev looks at me.

'Yes, but I'm visiting Helen this afternoon, so shall we make it at 7.30, or is that too early?'

We agree to meet at 7.30, Dev drives off to wherever he's going and Elias drops me off at my hotel.

I sit drinking coffee on the balcony going over the events of the past few days. Then I think of Dev. It sounds like he's a private investigator but then who does he work for and who are the 'other people' they both mentioned. Come to think of it, who are the people guarding Helen? Is it the police?

It's a lovely sunny day so before going to the hospital I take a walk to Voulis Street to buy some cakes for Helen, she has a very sweet tooth and loves Greek cakes.

A few minutes later, I'm walking along with my small box of baklava and galaktoboureko, two of her favourite cakes.

I can see my bus coming down the street and wave for it to wait for me, then run and jump inside.

I sit thinking about what Dev said about Helen being guarded 24-7. I'm so wrapped up in thinking about things that I miss my stop, I have to ask the bus driver to stop and let me out.

When I reach the hospital, I check to see where the security guards are. There's a guy dressed casually, standing not far from the back door reading a paper. He looks a bit obvious, I wonder if there are any more?

As I enter Helen's ward I can see a young woman

standing near the entrance, checking her cell phone. I watch her for a few minutes. She has one eye on her phone, and the other on the ward door.

She looks up suddenly and catches me watching her, I look away.

One of the nurses sees me and hurries over. 'Your friend opened her eyes, she didn't say anything, just looked at me then went back to sleep.'

I run to see Helen, she's asleep. I sit next to her and hold her hand. 'Helen, it's me, Beth. Squeeze my hand if you can hear me?' No response! Unperturbed, I sit chatting to her for a while, but she doesn't wake up.

An hour later I take the bus back to the hotel. On the way I hatch a plan for tonight. After dinner, I'll say I'm tired and leave. I'll find somewhere to wait until they leave, then I'll follow Dev. I have a feeling he works for MI6 or a similar organization, but I need to find out, my days of trusting people are long gone.

15

BETH

Dinner with Dev & Elias

Considering hardly anyone eats out until after 9.00pm in Athens, 7.30pm is very early.

As I draw near the restaurant, I can see the two of them on the terrace, they're seated some distance from the other diners on a small round table under a tree.

'Hi guys,' I murmur, as I walk onto the terrace.

Dev looks up from the menu he's scanning. 'Beth, come and sit down, we're trying to decide what to have for dinner.' He passes me the menu then lights a cigarette, inhales deeply and takes out his phone.

I wave away the smoke. 'You shouldn't smoke so much it's bad for you.'

He shrugs, changes his cigarette to the other hand and blows a ring of smoke up into the night air.

'Don't you smoke, sometimes, Beth?'

His blue eyes glint with amusement as he stubs out his cigarette.

'I used to smoke a lot, I might have a puff sometimes.'

He gives me a funny look, which makes me laugh - he probably thinks I smoke pot. 'I stick to wine and beer now, and the occasional brandy.'

The waiter comes over with his pad. 'Would you like to order?'

'What are we eating?' Dev asks, looking at us both.

'Lamb bizelli, for me,' Elias says. 'Sounds good, lamb with peas isn't it?'

The waiter nods.

'What about you, Beth?' Elias asks. 'There are lots of veggie things to choose from.'

'Are there any stuffed vegetables?'

Elias raises his eyebrows, in Greek which means no, Dev lights a cigarette.

'What about courgette fritters?' suggests Elias, 'I had them the other day, they were very good.'

'Great!' I look over at Dev, who is miles away, looking at his phone. He looks really stressed. Maybe something's happened?

Elias catches my eye and glances over at Dev and shrugs. 'Don't worry about him, he's got a lot on his mind, I'll order us a large Greek salad, a large French fries and a bottle of red wine. I think we all need it, don't you?'

I nod and lean back in my chair, now he's talking my language, this is just what I need, good company, good food and wine, and a relaxed atmosphere.

Soft Greek music plays in the background, Elias sits enjoying it, Dev's engrossed with his phone. I close my eyes for a moment and let the strains of the music flow over me, so romantic, so relaxing.

With a sigh I open my eyes and glance at the surrounding tables that glimmer with the glow of candles, all that's missing is Helen. Tears suddenly spring to my eyes. I quickly brush them away and catch Dev watching me.

The waiter arrives with a tray full of food which even Dev can't resist.

He scoops up a forkful of lamb, then another of potatoes and peas. 'I didn't realize I was so hungry,' he murmurs, taking another mouthful.

'You eat like a Greek,' Elias remarks, a satisfied grin on his face. 'How is your food, Beth?'

'Good! The fritters are delicious.'

After the meal the waiter brings us each a cup of Greek coffee, a small plate of loukoumia and three glasses of brandy, all on the house.

As soon as the waiter leaves Dev glances around at the nearby tables as if checking nobody can hear, then lowering his voice he leans forward. 'I've some interesting news for you both; remember the CCTV footage I told you about this morning? Well, I checked and it shows someone loitering around Helen's house on the afternoon just before the accident. Whoever it was lifted the hood of her car for a few seconds, then walked away.'

I lean across to take one of Dev's cigarettes, he pushes them closer to me and carries on talking.

'We don't have much to go on, he has a red cap pulled down over his head which covers most of his face, which doesn't help.'

'So, it could be a man or a woman,' Elias mutters, lighting one of his black tobacco cigarettes. 'What about the brakes? Could they have been cut from where this person was standing?'

Dev shrugs. 'Maybe.'

Elias sits puffing away on his cigarette, Dev's back on his phone. I stub out my cigarette and get up. 'Well guys I'm going to love you and leave you, I need an early night.' I wave to the waiter to bring the bill.

Dev frowns, 'It's on me.'

The waiter comes to the table, Dev hands him his card.

'Thanks,' I mutter. 'My turn next time, call me tomorrow?'

He nods.

They both offer to drive me back to the hotel, but I decline, thankfully they don't insist. I walk a little way down the street then cross over to a delicatessen I'd noticed earlier with a good view of the restaurant from inside.

Along one side of the shop is a fridge full of Greek sausages and cheeses, earthenware bowls full of yogurt, and pots of dips and all kinds of spreads. A box of crusty bread sits next to the till where the owners sits, and on the wall, opposite are colourful tins and jars of olives, bottles of wine, olive oil and other Greek food.

I pretend to be shopping, but my eyes are focused on the restaurant opposite the shop.

At last they come out. In my haste to hide behind a huge tin of feta cheese, I nearly knock over a box of oranges. The shop owner gives me a sharp look, I quickly straighten the box. 'What lovely oranges,' I mutter, the shop owner grunts, I walk over to the window.

They're chatting, then say goodbye and walk towards their cars.

Now what? I should have called a cab. Out of the corner of my eye I see a cab coming down the street.

I run out of the shop and wave it down. 'Follow that car,' I shout, pointing to Dev who's slowly pulling away.

The cab driver raises his eyebrows, grins and follows him.

He's heading in the direction of the Acropolis then he suddenly stops, parks on a side street and gets out of his car. He's in front of an old house, I quickly lean forward, pay the driver and duck down low.

I get out of the cab. The driver shakes his head, an amused look on his face and drives off. My eyes search the street and come back to the old mansion house he was standing in front of - where is he? I stand looking around, then realize he could be watching me, so walk behind a car. The old house seems to be boarded up, so he can't be in there.

I start walking back to the hotel, and on the way I try to Google the name of the street where Dev parked, but the street isn't marked, how strange.

Suddenly someone bumps into me nearly sending me flying.

'Hey, mind where you're going.'

Then I see it, a flash of steel, the blade of a knife, it's coming towards me. Instinctively, I jump away, he lunges towards me.

Someone shouts something in Greek - the man with the knife turns and runs.

A young Greek guy comes running over to me. 'Are you alright, did he hurt you?'

'No, I'm okay, but thanks for scaring him off, I really appreciate it.'

He points to my bag. 'Be careful, don't walk around the back streets, shall I walk with you?'

'No, it's okay, but thanks.'

He nods and walks off - I walk back to the main street. Was that a random attack? I walk quickly back to my hotel thinking about my attacker. He was dressed in black and wearing a black woolly hat, pulled down over his head, I didn't see his face.

I'm nearing the hotel when I think of Helen alone in that hospital. I wave down a cab and jump inside.

It's just gone 9.00 in the evening when I arrive at the hospital. Helen's asleep, the nurse is checking her. She looks at me in surprise. 'Is everything alright.'

'Yes, I just wanted to make sure she's okay.'

She smiles, finishes what she's doing then leaves us alone.

I forgot to see if the guards are still here.

I quickly take a peek outside and they're here. The same woman I saw earlier is near the ward, she suddenly looks over at me, then turns away.

With a sense of relief, I return to the ward. It's getting late so I tell Helen that I'll be back in the morning, she doesn't stir but maybe she heard me.

I'm outside the hospital when I get the feeling someone's watching me. I quickly hail a passing cab and slide inside. As I look out of the back window I see a car behind us.

As soon as we arrive at the hotel, I pay the driver, go straight to my room and without turning on the lights, peek through the shutters. It's the same car that was following me in the cab, it's too dark to see who's inside, but I can see the glimmer of a cigarette.

A few minutes pass then the car drives away.

Am I imagining it, or am I being followed?

16

DEV'S HEADQUARTERS

ATHENS

DEV SMILES to himself as he swipes his ID card to enter HQ, he knew Beth had followed him. He travels the thirty meters under street level and is soon met with the familiar sound of computers as the elevator doors slide open. Fresh air is piped in from other entrances around the Acropolis so he has no problem adjusting to the atmosphere.

Katia spots him and quickly comes over. 'Dev, how nice to see you.'

There's a definite hint of sarcasm in her voice but either he didn't hear her or he chooses to ignore it.

He starts flicking through some papers then passes the photo he just showed Beth and Elias to Katia. 'Can you get me a close-up of this photo, it's urgent.'

She shrugs.

'We don't have much to go on, Katia, so it would really help if you could do it now.'

She smiles and looks at the photo. 'But of course, Dev, anything for you.'

Although Katia's married, she recently had a short affair with Dev. She discovered her husband was cheating on her, she kicked him out and began a relationship with Dev. However, unbeknown to Dev, when her husband tired of screwing the girl, he wanted Katia back. She agreed to take him back, on the condition he didn't do it again - but she didn't tell Dev.

When Dev found out she'd taken her husband back, he ended the affair, as far as he was concerned, they were now just good friends. Katia on the other hand doesn't agree and wants their affair to continue.

He feels her brush against his hand as she leans over to take the photo. Her outward appearance is always professional, nobody guessed or knew of their affair.

'I'll be back later,' he says, moving out of her reach.

Katia walks to the other side of the room, an impish smile on her face.

An hour later, he's just about to leave HQ when his phone rings, he listens in silence, a worried look on his face. 'So, when did she leave the hospital?'

'It was after 10.00 tonight, she took a taxi back to the hotel.'

He knew Beth was worried about Helen, but she'd never visited her so late before. He's so engrossed with his thoughts that he doesn't realize Katia's standing next to him.

'I need to talk,' she says, a look of concern on her face. 'Can we meet later? It's important.'

She looks so worried, he immediately agrees. 'We can go

for a quick drink when I come back, but first I must visit forensics and the crime lab.'

She looks relieved and smiles. 'Good, give me a ring when you're here.'

He nods and leaves, his thoughts drift to Beth, he feels strangely drawn to her. He quickly snaps out of it and gets in his car.

IT'S NEARLY midnight when Dev returns to HQ, he's surprised to see that Katia's still there, he thought she'd have got tired of waiting.

'I thought you'd forgotten me,' she murmurs as soon as he comes in.

He grunts. 'It's very late, Katia, I thought you'd have left by now.'

He goes to his desk, grabs some papers and looks at her. 'Are you sure you still want to go for a drink?'

She nods.

Ten minutes later they're sitting together on a couch in a nearby bar.

'So, what's the problem?' he asks, tipping his beer into his mouth. He's thirsty and tired, he's had a long day.

'I'm not sure, but I think my husband is seeing another woman again.'

Dev knows she's lying, if her husband was carrying on with another woman, she'd have had him followed by now.

'Katia, I'm tired plus there's going to be a rally tomorrow afternoon, I'll have to have an early start to avoid it.'

'What's the rally for?'

He looks at her in amazement. 'Katia, the national healthcare system is understaffed and underfunded. Hospitals are unable to buy medical supplies and medicine, they are at breaking point.'

'Oh, of course I know about that, but what's the hurry?'

She leans close to him, her breast touches his hand. 'Stay and have a drink with me, it will help you relax, then you can drive me home.'

By home, he knows what she means and it isn't her home, it's his home.

He rolls his eyes. 'Katia, I have to go.' He knows this isn't what she wants to hear but he's tired. 'Look, I'll drop you off at your place if you like.'

She sits looking the other way ignoring him, he gets up and leaves.

As he slides into his car he takes out his phone and calls a department in HQ, he wants to know why Beth went to the hospital so late.

17

BETH

Athens - Plaka Hotel

Morning - 9.10 am

I grab my phone, it's nearly 9.00 in the morning, the sun's creeping through the blinds, I must call the hospital, see how Helen is.

I'm told she's okay but she hasn't opened her eyes again. The doctor suggests we visit her at separate times, talk to her, let her know we're there for her.

He's right, she needs something to wake up for - maybe if I can get Dev and Elias to visit her more often it might help.

My phone suddenly rings, it's Dev. I'm just about to tell him what the doctor said when I remember last night. The female guard probably told him about my late-night visit and now he's going to ask why I was there so late.

'Good morning Beth, if you're not too busy, can we meet somewhere today, around 2.00?'

I smile to myself, just as I thought. 'Yes, I'll come to your office, what's the address?'

Now what's he going to say?

He hesitates, then starts prattling on about how busy he is. 'I'll be out most of the day, how about we meet at the same café in Syntagma Square as we did the other day?'

Just as I thought, he doesn't want me to know where his office is.

'Okay, but first I'm going to the hospital, I just called the doctor and he said...'

'Sorry, but can you tell me later Beth, I'll see you at 2.00 in the square.'

I'm just about to say yes but he's already hung up.

On the way to the bus stop I think of last night, the guy with the knife and the car outside the hotel. I wave down a passing cab and twenty minutes later I'm at the hospital.

Another woman's guarding the ward door today, I can't help wondering who's paying for all this. It can't be the police guarding Helen 24 – 7 - so who's paying for it?

I turn and hurry to the ward, Helen's just the same as when I saw her last night, she looks so peaceful, I squeeze her hand gently.

'Helen, you must wake up, please wake up!' Almost immediately she opens her eyes, smiles then closes them. 'Helen, it's me, wake up,' I almost shout but it's no use. Just as I'm about to call for the doctor a nurse comes running in.

'Are you alright?' she asks, looking at me then at Helen.

'She just opened her eyes, I ...'

She gives me a reassuring smile. 'This is good, I'll let the doctor know.'

After about an hour I check to see if the guards are still there, they are.

Ten minutes later I'm on the bus going to meet Dev.

THE BUS ARRIVES at Syntagma Square just after 2.00, Dev's already on the terrace of the café.

'You look happy,' he murmurs, as soon as I sit down. 'Has something happened?'

He's right. I seem to have a permanent smile on my face which is unusual for me, especially after the last few days.

He peers at me expectantly. 'So, what happened?'

'I went to see Helen; she opened her eyes and she smiled at me!'

His eyebrows shoot up. 'Wow! Did she say anything?'

'No, it was so quick. She opened her eyes, smiled and then closed them. I sat and talked to her but she didn't wake up. As you know the doctor said it helps so I was thinking, maybe...'

Dev smiles. 'I know what you're going to say, that we could pay one of the nurses to sit with her and talk to her.'

'No Dev, they've enough to do, we can't ask them, but if we could take it in turns...'

He looks surprised, and then smiles. 'If you think it will help, I can squeeze in a few minutes this afternoon, but I have no idea what I'm going to talk about.'

I laugh. 'Who cares, as long as you're there.' I'm so happy, I could hug him. 'Read her something from a magazine or a newspaper, don't read her the news, read something nice, something to make her want to wake up.'

A waiter appears and we order coffee. After he's gone, I turn to Dev wondering if I should tell him about last night. I need to know who he's working for, why the hell can't he just tell me?

I take a sip of water from my bottle to clear my throat and begin. 'Dev, I have a confession to make.' Then I stop, maybe he already knows? He's not stupid. Maybe he saw me getting out of the cab, that's why he disappeared so quickly.

He raises an eyebrow, looking mildly surprised and do I see a glint of amusement in his eyes? Shit, did he see me in the cab last night? I'm about to tell him when he starts laughing.

'What's so funny?' I ask, glaring at him.

He suddenly becomes serious. 'Look Beth, I know things probably don't make sense but I'm definitely legit, so don't worry.'

'But I am worried, Dev. James is dead, someone tried to kill Helen and...'

I stop and bite my lip. I was going to tell him about the guy last night, the one with the knife, not a good idea.

'Look, all I want to know is who you work for? Why is it all such a big mystery? And who's footing the bill for the guards at the hospital? It can't be the police.'

He sighs deeply, looks away for a few seconds, then leans forward. 'Beth, have you heard of the secret underground tunnels in Athens?'

'Of course, the caves and underground passages from ancient times, they're all over Athens.'

He nods and makes a flourishing movement, gesturing with his hand to the Grand Bretagne Hotel behind us. 'When the Nazis occupied Greece, Hitler made the Grand Bretagne Hotel their headquarters. There are underground tunnels all over Athens which have been used by many over the years. The area around the Acropolis is full of caves and sanctuaries, many with natural water. There are the caves on the East face and many more on the North face. On the South slope, behind the temple of Asklepios, is a Russian Church built into the rock.'

I'm amazed he knows so much, but why is he telling me this? Why on earth is he talking about the bloody tunnels? Maybe he's just interested, I wonder if he's heard about the tunnels in Vouliagmeni?

I look at him and smile. 'I know all about the tunnels Dev, don't forget I used to live here. Did you know there's an underwater cave in Vouliagmeni? There are tunnels all over Athens maybe you'd like to visit some one day?'

He smiles, I think he's enjoying it, but he hasn't answered my question.

He lights a cigarette and leans back in his chair. 'I know Vouliagmeni, it's a lovely place, there's a beautiful beach, I often go to the thermal spa, it has healing properties...'

I wonder what he needs healing? Maybe an old wound, if he works for MI6 that's quite possible.

I nod. 'Yes, Athens airport used to be close to the beach, just west of Glyfada. It was called Ellinikon Airport, it was much easier to get to from where we lived, and we could easily see Vouliagmeni lake when the plane was landing at the airport. Of course that was some time ago.'

He smiles and sips his coffee, I carry on talking.

'There's also an underwater cave at the edge of the lake that has never been fully explored, there are fourteen tunnels one of which is 800 metres long, the longest in the world.'

'It's really quite amazing isn't it?' he says, watching me intently. 'There's an entire city beneath Athens with ancient secrets hidden from view - caves, holy shrines, churches, deep wells, long underground passages.'

I nod.

He carries on. 'During times of war they were used to get to places quickly, other times they were just a way of transporting things to other parts of Athens.'

'And the house you visited last night?' I ask, holding my breath.

He looks up quickly, laughs and takes another sip of coffee. 'Yes, Beth, as you saw last night it's just one of many such places in Athens, there are so many, aren't there?'

I don't say anything, what can I say? I had a feeling he'd seen me, so where did he disappear to?

He takes out a cigarette, lights it, inhales deeply, then looks at me thoughtfully. 'This is where we have our headquarters, it has to be somewhere safe, so we chose one of the very old mansion houses which are no longer used. It was easy to convert to modern offices and it's in the centre of town, just where we need it.' He hesitates for a few minutes. 'I work for the government in the UK.'

I say nothing, he carries on talking.

'There are others working with me in the fight against crime and terrorism.'

'So, these are the *other people* Elias was talking about?'

'Yes, James asked if I could help Helen, she was going through a tough time, so of course I obliged. I have the resources, so it was easy to put her husband under surveillance.'

'How many people work with you?'

'In this office there are about ten of us.' He looks very serious and lowers his voice. 'Look Beth, it's going to start getting nasty, so I suggest you leave it to me from now on, I'll keep you up to date with what's happening.'

I can't believe what he just said. Does he really think I frighten off so easily? He doesn't know about my past activities, if he did, he'd never say this. Maybe I should enlighten him on what I can do?

I smile. 'Don't worry about me, I can look after myself, I've lots of experience.'

For a second he looks surprised, he raises his eyebrows, then in a serious voice adds. 'Beth, think carefully about what I've said. Now I really must go, shall I walk you back to your hotel?'

'No, I've some things to do. Call me if you have any news... and don't forget to see Helen and tell Elias.'

He nods, he's just about to leave when he turns and looks at me. 'Why did you go to the hospital so late last night?'

I knew it, that's why he really wanted to see me today. He wants to know what I'm up to, he's a control freak.

'I wanted to see Helen, why?'

He looks at me and frowns. 'But it was so late, did something happen?'

Does he know about the guy who attacked me? He seems to know everything. Shit, has he got someone following me?

I look at him and shrug. 'No, I just wanted to see her.' I know he doesn't believe me, I can see it in his eyes.

'Okay, well I have to go, I'll call you later.'

I watch him walk back to his car. 'Don't forget to go to the hospital and talk to Helen,' I call.

He turns and nods, then carries on walking.

18

DEV

Later that afternoon

Dev smiles to himself as he walks the short distance to where his car is parked. It's unusual for someone to be as inquisitive as Beth. On a case like this it's important to know what makes people tick, she probably has nothing to hide, but he should check her out, just to be sure.

Dev studied criminal law and trained as a journalist, he worked in the Middle East and Europe and ended up working for the government. The human mind fascinates him. He works with like-minded people and has contacts all over the world.

Flicking his key fob the car springs into action, he slides into the black convertible BMW and drives to the hospital.

He parks and walks to the entrance, checks to make sure the guards are where they should be, they are. Her room's just off the main ward; pulling up a chair he talks to her for five minutes. He chats about seeing Beth earlier, then stops, it seems ridiculous talking to someone who's not responding. He has another go and tells her about the restaurant they all went to the other night. He stands up and says he's going for a walk to stretch his legs.

In the centre of the ward there's a table piled high with magazines and newspapers. Thinking he might find something of interest to read Helen, he begins flicking through the pages of a local Greek magazine. A photograph of a young man coming out of one of the law courts catches his eye. Even more interesting is the woman standing next to him, its James's wife, Isabelle. He scans the article - the man she's with is out on bail awaiting trial for smuggling drugs.

After taking a note of the magazine he returns to Helen's room. He pulls up a chair and whispers in her ear. 'I've just found something very important, Helen, I must go, see you tomorrow.'

When he's out of the hospital, he sends a text to a friend who lives not far from the hospital, he might be able to help, then he walks towards his car.

He's just opening his car door, when a text comes through.

Hi Dev, I'm at home, come round, look forward to seeing you. Zeph

Zeph lives in Kiffissia, one of the most exclusive areas of Athens. Many of the houses are surrounded by high walls or hedges with CCTV and security gates. As he nears Zeph's house he slows down, parks and walks the few yards to the house. He presses the intercom at the side of a large dark wooden door. A few seconds later the door opens. Inside is a huge garden surrounded by pine trees, fauna and flowers. At the far end of the garden is a large swimming pool, in the centre is a beautiful house, pink bougainvillea cascades down the walls.

His friend Zeph, short for Zepheros, walks out of the house carrying a jar of freshly squeezed orange juice and a couple of glasses.

'Over here Dev,' he calls, pointing to a round wooden table on the shaded terrace.

Dev walks over and sits on one of the comfortable looking sage green chairs, Zeph is an old friends, they often work together and enjoy each other's company. The lovely house and garden are the result of Zeph's hard work.

After bringing Zeph up to date with the horrendous events of the last few days, Dev tells him about the article he found in the magazine.

Zeph removes his sunglasses and scans the article Dev shows him on his phone.

After a few minutes he turns to Dev. 'I've heard about this case. The man they're talking about in that article was caught smoking hashish, he said he'd bought some for a smoke, trouble is he seems to be in the country illegally. After checking him out they found his place full of the stuff. I think the woman next to him is his sister.'

Dev raises an eyebrow. 'Any idea when the trial is?'

'In a few days, I think. I'll let you know for sure later today if you like. Has this got something to do with the recent events?'

Dev nods. 'I'm not sure but it's worth checking.'

He knew he could rely on Zeph to be up to date on this sort of thing, they'd studied law together in the UK and still work together on some cases. After working in London for some time with Dev, Zeph returned to Greece and became a successful lawyer.

Dev smiles at his old friend. 'Thanks, we need all the help we can get.'

Zeph walks with him to the garden gate. 'Come round more often, it's nice to see you out of work. Maybe this weekend if you're not too busy, we can have dinner here or try one of the local tavernas.'

'Yes, that would be nice, but I don't think it will be possible this weekend.'

He opens the gate and turns to Zeph. 'Call me if you find out anything.'

A few minutes later Dev's driving back to HQ.

19

BETH

ATHENS, Plaka Hotel
Early morning

THE HOTEL PHONE'S RINGING, I let it ring. To my annoyance it rings again. Who can it be? Nobody calls me on this phone.

Sticking my hand out, I grope for it on the bedside table. 'Yes,' I groan, sleepily.

'Good morning, sorry to wake you, but I need to talk to you.'

I'm suddenly wide awake, I don't recognize the voice, it's not the hospital, so who is it?

I glance at my phone – 5.45 in the morning. 'Who is it?' I mumble, wishing I hadn't answered.

'I have something to tell you.'

His voice is low and for some reason it makes my skin crawl.

'It's about your friend, James.'

I shoot out of bed. 'Who is this?' I demand, walking over to the window and peeping out. I have no idea why I'm doing this, but I instinctively feel he's outside, not in the hotel.

'It doesn't matter who I am, this is urgent.'

I need to put a trace on this.

'How did you know I was at this hotel?'

'Many people know you stay at this hotel when you come here. You used to live in Athens and many people follow you on social media.' He laughs, a nasty horrible laugh. 'Don't worry, you can trust me, I want to help.'

My mind's racing, how does he know this? I must delay him, I'll call Dev.

'Hold on for a second, I need to go to the bathroom.'

'No, it must be now, give me your cell phone number or I won't call you back.'

Shit! He must have guessed what I'm thinking. I feel like slamming the phone down, but I don't. I want to know who he is.

There's no time to call Dev, so I give him my number.

He calls back immediately.

'You must listen carefully and not say a word about this to anyone.'

I sit on the bed, my phone close to my ear, listening to his soft creepy voice.

'Your friend was collateral damage. You must stop putting your nose into things that don't concern you. This is the last time I am telling you, do you understand?'

'Who killed him and why?' I shout, gripping my phone tightly. 'He may just be collateral damage to you, but he was my friend and I want to know why he was killed.'

'I'm not going to say this anymore. You must go back to London and forget about this, otherwise...'

'Otherwise what? Are you threatening me?'

'If you value your safety, leave Greece now.'

'Who the hell are you?' I shout, angrily.

But he's hung up. He only spoke for a minute, he's being careful. I quickly call Dev but it goes to voicemail. I leave a message telling him it's urgent, and to call me back.

A minute later my phone rings, it's Dev, he sounds as if he's just woken up.

'I need to see you now, I just had a weird call from someone, it's about James.'

'I'm coming,' he mutters. 'I'll be there soon.'

20

DEV & BETH

Athens, Plaka Hotel
Early morning 5.55 am

I open the balcony door to the early morning sounds of Athens, it's one of my favourite times of the day, everything's so new, it's like the slate has been wiped clean for another day.

The street vendors are already at work setting up stalls to sell the popular round sesame bread rings. People are rushing off to work, tourists are arriving and leaving, and I desperately need a strong hot coffee.

After splashing my face with water, I pull on a pair of trousers and head for the hotel terrace.

Nobody's here yet so I have my pick of tables. The early morning sun spreads a glow of warmth across the city as I sit thinking of what just happened.

A waiter appears and takes my order.

A minute later he returns with my coffee. 'Up early today?' he asks, grinning at my disheveled appearance.

I nod, realizing I haven't brushed my hair and still have my nightshirt on.

'What about some toast?'

'No thanks, maybe later.'

He goes off and I sit thinking about the man who just phoned me. I haven't really kept in contact with anybody here since I left, except of course Helen and James.

'Good morning Beth,' Dev pulls up a chair and sits down beside me. He smells fresh and clean, how does he do it? I turn and look at him. Gray suit, white shirt, just a little bit of stubble – amazing!

'I'm OK,' I reply, sipping my coffee. 'It takes more than a creep like that to frighten me. What worries me is Helen.'

Dev orders a coffee and for a few minutes we sit in silence, we're both waiting until the waiter brings his drink.

'Can we trace the number?' I suddenly ask, unable to wait any longer.

'I've already done that. He was calling you from a phone box outside the metro in Monesteraki, we're checking to see if there's CCTV in the area.'

The waiter returns with his coffee and another for me.

Dev takes a few gulps, then turns and looks at me. 'Tell me everything this man said.'

I relate our conversation as best I can. Dev stiffens when I come to the bit about – *if I value my safety, I must leave Greece* – and starts drumming his fingers on the table.

'Do you have any idea who he is?' he asks, peering at me. 'If we know what he looks like, we can check him out and see if he belongs to any of the political organizations in Athens.'

I shake my head.

'It must be political,' he mutters to himself. 'Why else would he tell you to stop putting your nose into things that don't concern you.'

He stops for a moment and frowns. 'Are you politically active? Do you belong to a party or an organization in Greece or London?'

I'm amazed he should ask this. 'What does that have to do with it?'

'Come on, Beth, you're a journalist, you know what I'm talking about.'

I shrug. 'I studied politics and economics here at uni in Athens.'

'Anything else?'

He sits watching me closely, what else does he want to know, who I voted for?

'I need to know everything, Beth, if you want me to find him.'

'Well, as a student I was quite political, who isn't? I learnt to look after myself. Mum got me to take martial arts lessons.' I don't tell him why I learnt martial arts and how to use a gun, that's got nothing to do with this and will only waste time.

I start thinking back to my days at uni, all the friends and people we knew. Then a strange thing happens, I sit staring at Dev, amazed that I didn't realize it before. It must have been his hair or his clothes that threw me, he's changed, but...

'What's wrong, Beth?'

'I know who it was,' I mutter. 'How on earth could I forget him.'

Dev stares at me in surprise. 'So, you know who this man is?'

'No, I'm not talking about the guy who called me this morning.'

For a minute he looks confused. 'So, who are you talking about.'

'It happened the day James...' I swallow and carry on. 'I was having a drink in a café near the Acropolis, a man came and sat next to me, he said he knew me.'

Dev looks at me sharply.

'I had no idea who he was, he gave me the creeps, I told him he was mistaken and left.'

Dev leans back in his chair looking puzzled.

I sit shaking my head. 'I just remembered who he is, he was a student at uni.'

Dev's looking at me strangely, how stupid I must sound he has no idea what I'm talking about, why should he?

I shrug, wishing I hadn't said anything. 'It was a long time ago when I was at uni in Athens, this guy always gave me the creeps, he used to annoy Alex as well.'

'Who's Alex?'

'My husband, we're divorced now.'

'How did you meet him?'

'Who, my ex?'

He nods.

'At university, in Athens.'

'Do you still see him?'

'No.'

He's the last person I want to see, but I'm not going to tell Dev that.

'Where is he now?' he asks.

'Probably still in Athens?' Why does he want to know, what has he got to do with anything?

'So, you haven't seen him since your divorce?'

'No, I just told you, the last time we spoke was a few

months ago. He was in London, he called to see if I had the telephone number of someone we knew at uni.

'What does your ex do?'

'He's a lawyer.'

'You didn't see him in London?'

'No,' I reply, wondering why he's asking so many questions. He has a strange look in his eyes. I sit waiting for him to say something, he quickly looks away, takes out his phone and reads a text.

'It's time for me to go, Beth.' He slips his phone back in his pocket and stands up. 'Let me know if you need anything.' He walks over to the elevator and is gone.

I sit gazing after him then return to my room for a quick shower before I see Helen.

ON MY WAY to the bus stop I buy a takeaway coffee and a cake for Helen.

As I enter the hospital a nurse rushes up to me nearly knocking me over.

'I saw you from the window,' she pants, sounding out of breath. 'I have good news for you, your friend, she's awake. Come, I will take you to her.'

'Wow!' I stand staring at her in surprise.

'Come on.' She grabs my arm and walks with me to the ward.

Then I hear a familiar voice.

'Beth.'

It's Helen, she's sitting up in bed smiling at me.

I stand staring at her for a few seconds, then run over and gently put my arms around her. 'Oh Helen, it's so good to see you, how do you feel?'

'I'm OK, just a bit weak, but fine. What about you? What's been happening?'

I start updating her with all the news, then I quickly call Dev to let him know Helen's awake.

An hour later, as I'm leaving, I get the feeling someone's following me. I begin walking quickly. I can't see any taxis. I know a bus is due but they're often late. Shit, shall I go back to the hospital?

Just then a bus turns the corner, I run to get it, the doors shut behind me, I quickly walk to the back of the bus.

Out of the back window I can see a man with a hooded top pulled over his face. It's the same man who followed me the other evening from the restaurant, the one with the knife.

When I reach Syntagma, I get off the bus and walk quickly to my hotel, I must keep my wits about me, someone is following me and they're up to no good.

At the hotel I drink a small bottle of brandy, flop on the bed, and close my eyes.

What time is it?

I stretch, slide off the sofa and pad over to the window. It's dark outside, then I realize I'm hungry, I feel I need something nutritious, I've had enough cheese pies to last me a lifetime. I glance at the hotel menu, the stuffed peppers look good, I'll call room service.

After a quick shower, I flick on the TV.

There's a tap at the door. It's my food.

With the tray perched on my lap I sit eating and watching the news. The stuffed peppers are good, I should have ordered more. I glance over at the TV and gasp - the food falls from my fork.

James's wife, Isabelle is on the TV with a young guy. I can't rewind the footage and curse myself for not watching it properly. No wonder she didn't let us know when the funeral was, who the hell is this guy, and why is she on the news?

I try calling Dev but he's not picking up, so I leave a message to call me urgently.

He doesn't call back, so I order a bottle of wine and fall asleep watching a film.

I CAN HEAR my phone ringing. 'Yes,' I mumble, sleepily.

'Beth, I'm sorry to call you so late, I really didn't want to, but we need your help.'

It's Dev, I struggle to sit up, my mouth's dry and I feel like shit. 'What are you talking about?'

I pad over to the small hotel fridge and look for something cold to drink.

Why did I have that third class of wine.

'Can you come to the casino?' he asks.

'What! Are you crazy?'

'No, I'm not crazy,' he snaps. 'It's about the man who called you this morning. I think I've identified him, I've been following him all day. I checked the CCTV footage outside the metro at Monesteraki, around the time he called you, I want you to see if you recognize him.'

'But I've never met him, Dev. I don't know who he is.'

'I know, but this is all we have to go on.'

The TV's still on in the background, I quickly turn it off.

'Why don't you get *your people* to take a photo of him and send it to me,' I groan. 'What's the point of going to the casino when I can see it on my phone?'

'I knew you'd say that, I'm sending it right now, let me know if you recognize him.'

I look at the photo, one has a beard, he has a black flat cap on and is wearing dark glasses. How the hell can I recognize someone from this? The other guy is bald with a pinched looking face and owl-like glasses.

'Sorry Dev, I've no idea who they are.'

'I thought you'd say that,' he replies, rather abruptly. 'That's why I asked you to come to the casino to see them in person. I'll be outside your hotel in about fifteen minutes.'

I can't believe it! What's he playing at? Of course, I want to know who called me, but this is ridiculous. I groan and haul myself into the bathroom, splash my face with water, brush my teeth and find something to wear to the casino.

My hair looks terrible, I clip it up on top of my head. I'm wearing my little black dress, it's perfect for a night at the casino. Now where are my boots?

My phone rings, it's Dev. 'Hurry, I'm downstairs.'

Grabbing my coat and bag, I quickly slip on my boots and leave my room.

The elevator's there, I run and jump inside, Dev 's waiting outside, I walk over and slide into his car.

Twenty minutes later, we're at the lower teleferique station. We park then go inside and into a waiting cable car.

It only takes seven minutes and we're outside the casino. After paying the entrance fee we make our way to the bar. Dev orders a beer for both of us.

'They're sitting on your right, about ten feet away,' he mumbles.

I spot them immediately, they're deep in conversation, we sit drinking in silence, I try and observe them without making it look too obvious.

Suddenly a woman bumps into Dev, practically

knocking him off his stool, his beer goes flying and he just saves himself from falling by hanging onto the bar.

'*Signomi, signomi* - sorry, sorry,' the woman says in a husky, Melina Mercouri type voice. 'I will get you another - barman, barman, give him another beer.'

The barman grabs a beer and starts pouring it into a glass in front of Dev. The woman leans across Dev, shoving her ample breasts in his face and starts wiping the beer off his jacket.

Dev gently pushes her hand away. 'Don't worry, I can manage.'

The woman leans back, gives his jacket another dab, pays the barman for the drink, then disappears back into the casino.

'That livened things up for you, didn't it?' I say, trying not to laugh.

He glares at me, then looks over to where the men are sitting. 'I think the weedy looking one with the owlish glasses has gone.'

I take a quick peek and he's right, he has gone. The other guy's looking at his phone, I can't see his face because of his hat, his beard and his dark glasses. Then he stands up as if to leave, he's tall and slim, his clothes look expensive, do I know him? I sit watching him closely.

Dev starts groaning, then he falls to the floor clutching his stomach.

'Dev!' I jump off my stool and squat down beside him. 'What's wrong?'

'I don't feel good,' he groans, pulling up his knees and holding his stomach.

'Get a doctor,' I shout, looking at the barman. 'Can someone please get a doctor.'

The barman jumps, then grabs a phone.

A few minutes later a doctor arrives, he takes one look at Dev and mutters, 'We must get him to hospital immediately, he's in a lot of pain, we'll take my car.'

A couple of men at the bar stand watching us.

The doctor walks over to them. 'Don't just stand there, help me.'

They try to pick Dev up but he's in so much pain it's difficult - the doctor yells to the barman to get a chair from the reception area with wheels.

A few minutes later a chair is brought to the bar. Dev's placed as gently as possible into the chair, then the doctor wheels him outside to the car park.

Eventually we get him in the back seat of the doctor's car, I climb in beside him, the doctor drives like a maniac down the mountain road, I groan inwardly.

At every turn the car makes Dev falls over me. Soon we're off the mountain road heading for the central Athens. Suddenly the doctor puts on his brakes, the car squeals to a halt outside the hospital, he leaps out and runs inside.

A few minutes later he returns with a nurse wheeling a chair.

'Help me get him in the chair,' he yells to me.

Very gently we ease Dev out of the car and into the chair, then he's wheeled into a room to be examined.

I sit outside holding my head in my hands, I knew this was a bad idea, why the hell did I say I would come?

A few minutes later someone coughs.

I look up, there's a doctor peering at me.

'I've just examined your friend, he's been poisoned, we're going to pump his stomach.'

'Oh my God, poisoned? Will he be alright?'

He nods. 'Yes, he should feel better in the morning.'

I quickly call Elias, there's no reply, I leave a message.

Helen's in the same hospital as Dev, so I pop out the back to see if the guards are still there, they are.

Back in the emergency room I find a policewoman waiting for me. She leads me into a small side room with a desk and a couple of chairs. She motions for me to sit down opposite her. 'Do you remember anything unusual happening this evening?'

I shrug. 'No not really.'

She's watching me closely now. 'Were you sitting alone when this happened?

'We were having a drink at the bar, that's all. A woman bumped into him, knocked his drink all over him...'

The officer raises an eyebrow. 'Did she do anything else?'

'She apologized profusely, in fact I think she overdid it.' I pause and look at her. 'Oh no...'

'Yes,' she says, shaking her head. 'It was no accident, this is how they work. It was a distraction so they could...'

'She poisoned his drink?'

The officer nods.

Of course, she did it - I remember her leaning over Dev to brush his jacket. That's when she did it. Or was it the barman who popped it into the beer?

'We have to check the CCTV footage above the bar,' the officer murmurs. 'The casino is full of cameras, so we have a lot to go on.'

She takes down my details, phone number, name of the hotel I'm staying at, then leaves. I'm so tired I take a cab back to my hotel. I'll see Helen and Dev tomorrow.

21

DEV

ATHENS CENTRAL HOSPITAL

DEV SLOWLY OPENS HIS EYES. Then it all comes back to him.

The casino, Beth.

He tries to sit up but falls back.

'Don't move,' a nurse calls, running over to him. 'We had to pump your stomach out last night.'

'Beth - the woman who was with me, is she okay?'

'Yes, she is fine,' the nurse replies, smiling. 'Now try and relax.'

Taking a glass of water from the bedside table she helps him drink, then leaves.

Dev lays in bed looking at the ceiling trying to remember what happened.

He tries sitting up but falls back again, the nurse comes rushing over.

'I told you to relax you must get your strength back. You can phone your friend later, for now you must try to rest, the doctor will be here soon to see you.'

BETH

I SET my alarm for 7.00am and wake up sweating.

Dev! I grab my phone. No missed calls.

I call the hospital, they say he's okay, but still a bit weak, he'll be out later today.

After a quick shower I leave for the hospital.

When I arrive I see Helen's nurse chatting to another nurse, she spots me and runs over.

'Quickly, the doctor wants to see you!'

'What happened?' I gasp, staring at her.

'Nothing,' she says, laughing. 'Come with me.'

The doctor smiles as I enter his office. 'Good morning Beth have you heard the good news?'

I know Helen's awake but so do they, so I shake my head.

'What happened?'

The doctor's beaming at me. 'Helen, she can leave hospital today.'

'But isn't it a bit early?'

'No, she needs to be with her family and friends.'

I go to say something, he stops me.

'Don't worry, the nurse will help Helen get ready, I believe your friend is here in another ward.'

'Yes, I'm just going to see him, but are you sure...'

He shakes his head. 'Now go and see your friend while Helen gets ready.'

When I get to Dev's ward I'm surprised to see him propped up in bed, he looks relieved to see me.

'Morning Dev, how are you?'

He pulls a face. 'Still a bit groggy, they want to keep me in until this afternoon.'

'Don't worry,' I murmur, going over to the bed. 'You'll soon be out of here.'

A doctor comes into the ward followed by a nurse who comes over to me.

'Are you Beth?'

I nod.

She looks over at Dev. 'He's been asking about you, he's been very worried.'

'I couldn't remember what happened,' he mutters.

The doctor starts drawing the curtain around the bed. 'I'll only be a few minutes, you can wait outside.'

I leave them to it and find somewhere quiet to sit, I'll give Elias a call.

A few minutes later the doctor comes to find me. 'Your friend's doing well,' he announces, happily. 'He can leave later today.'

'Thanks, can I see him?'

'But of course.'

Dev and I start chatting about last night, then he asks about Helen.

'They just told me she's well enough to leave but it seems very quick.' I lower my voice. 'If she does leave, I'll need to find somewhere safe for her to stay.'

'Don't worry. I'll talk to the hospital and police. Let me know when you're back at the hotel, we have a lot to talk about.'

I'm just about to go when he suddenly asks. 'What did the police say to you last night?'

I've a feeling he won't like what I'm about to say, and I'm right. When I get to the bit about the woman bumping into him and how the police said this is how criminal gangs work, he rolls his eyes and groans.

'Are they checking the CCTV footage above the bar and in the casino?'

'Yes, do you think the barman was in on it?'

He shrugs, suddenly he looks worried. 'We'll talk about it later, but for now we must look after Helen.' As an afterthought, he adds. 'It might be better if she stays in for a few more days, ask the doctor and see what he says?'

'Okay, but I don't think he'll agree, they need the beds.'

He looks tired, so I leave him to rest and go in search of the doctor.

He's outside the front entrance, smoking. We chat for a while about the political situation in Greece, then I casually ask. 'Don't you think it would be better if Helen stays in for a few more days? She's still very weak and needs to recover.'

'As long as she takes it easy, she will soon be back to normal,' he says, stubbing out his cigarette on the ground with his shoe. 'Being in here will not help, she needs lots of fresh air.' He looks at me and murmurs. 'As you know we are stretched to the limit, resources are low and...'

'I know things are bad in Greece right now, and you've all been so good to Helen.'

He smiles. 'We do our best, now if you will excuse me I must get back to work.'

I make a mental note to add this to the article I'm writing about the situation in Greece.

OF COURSE, Helen's over the moon to be out of hospital. I booked a cab so there's no waiting around. She stands looking up at the sky enjoying the sun on her face, then slides slowly into the cab.

Half an hour later we're enjoying coffee and biscuits in our rooms at the hotel.

'It's great to be back,' she says, putting her mug of coffee on the side table. 'I've really missed this place.' She snuggles back under her duvet, then a knock at the door makes us jump.

'Beth, it's me.'

Helen laughs, I run to the door.

'Dev!'

I lower my voice so Helen won't hear me. 'I was coming to collect you later, how did you get here?' I stand staring at him, he looks so pale. 'Are you sure you're well enough to leave hospital?'

He looks at me and grins. 'Of course.' Then lowering his voice, he adds. 'Elias collected me, he wanted to come in and see you both, but you know what it's like, he has another demonstration to cover...'

'Yes, I saw it on the news'

Then I grab his arm and pull him inside. 'Don't stand in the doorway.'

'Look, I don't want to disturb you, I just wanted to check that you're alright, have you heard from the police?'

Then he notices Helen, trying to sit up in bed behind me.

'Helen!' he exclaims, walking over to her bed. 'How are you?'

He helps me prop her up with some pillows then sits next to her. We chat for a while. Dev gives her updates on what's been happening, leaving last night out of course, that would only upset her.

We order pizza from room service. Helen looks more like her old self and Dev has a bit of colour in his cheeks.

Suddenly Dev stands up. 'Well thanks for the pizza, now I really must go, I have some things to do.'

'I'll call reception and get you a cab.'

He turns to Helen who's already half asleep. 'It's good to have you back with us, Helen.'

She nods, then snuggles down under the duvet.

'There's a cab downstairs, Dev, do you want it?'

'Yes.'

I walk him to the door. He turns and in a low voice says. 'I'll call you later, Beth, and don't worry, we'll work something out.'

I nod. 'You need to rest when you get home.'

He smiles and closes the door.

I wave to him from the balcony and watch as his cab drives away.

'Shit, I forgot to tell him about...'

'Tell him what?'

Shit! I thought she was asleep. Why did I say that? Now is not the time to tell her I saw James's wife on TV with a young guy.

Helen's looking at me sleepily. 'What did you forget, Beth?'

'I forgot to say... we might be doing something tomorrow, that is if you feel like it, we can go to a restaurant near the beach, maybe Elias will take us, the sea air will do you good.'

Helen beams with delight, 'What a wonderful idea.'

I make her comfortable then go onto the balcony and call Elias.

'Hi Elias, I just wanted to let you know that Helen's back at the hotel with me and Dev's just left to go home.'

'Yes, sorry I didn't call you earlier to let you know about Dev.'

'It doesn't matter, but there's something I need to tell you about Helen. The doctor said she needs to get lots of fresh air, so I thought we might have lunch at the beach tomorrow.'

'Are you sure?'

'Yes, she's looking forward to it.'

He grunts. 'Okay, if you're sure she's well enough, I'll take you in my car.'

22

HELEN

ATHENS, *Plaka Hotel*
Next Day - Breakfast Time

HELEN'S ON THE BALCONY, there's a slight breeze but it's still sunny, she shivers slightly.

'Let's go for a drive to Mont Parnes instead of the beach, we can take the teleferique and have lunch. What do you think?'

I inwardly groan. 'But I thought we were going to the beach? It's not as warm as usual but we can wrap up.'

'I don't want to risk it. The doctor said I need fresh air, but I don't want to catch a cold. If we go to Mont Parnes, we'll be inside most of the time. Don't worry Beth, I'm fine, I just need to go out, I've been in bed for so long.'

My phone rings, it's Elias, I walk back to the room so Helen won't hear me. 'She's changed her mind,' I hiss, holding my hand over the mouthpiece so she won't hear me. 'She wants to go to Mont Parnes, not the beach.'

'What! Have you forgotten what happened?'

'I know, I'm worried too, but she can't stay here all day, she needs fresh air, she really wants to go.' I lower my voice to a whisper. 'I haven't told her about Dev, so don't say anything when you see her.'

He's silent, so I carry on.

'Maybe if we disguise ourselves it'll be alright, they're not after you Elias so while we're there you can find out about the other night, you're a journalist they'll speak to you.'

He doesn't sound too happy. 'It's not so easy, Beth.'

'Oh come on Elias, you've nothing to lose, don't you want to know who poisoned Dev? The police are checking the CCTV cameras in the casino, so while we're there you can...

He grunts. 'Okay, I'll try but I'm worried...' He hesitates for a moment. 'What if someone recognizes you, what will you wear?'

'I'm going to Ermou Street, it's only a couple of minutes from here, there are so many shops, I'll find something.'

He gives a dry laugh. 'You should both wear wigs and masks.'

'Yeah, right, talk to you later.' Sarcastic bugger, but maybe it's not such a bad idea, Helen hates wigs but she'll just have to put up with it.

Helen looks up when I come back onto the balcony.

'Did you arrange it?' she asks, there's a twinkle in her eyes, and I know she was listening, I hope she didn't hear the bit about Dev.

'Yes, Elias is driving us to the teleferique and from there

we'll take the cable car to Mont Parnes. But are you sure it's not too much for you?'

'I'll be sitting down most of the time so of course it'll be okay.'

'I know you won't like this, but we must disguise ourselves, just to be on the safe side.'

She raises an eyebrow. 'Don't you think that's being a bit dramatic?'

I look at her in amazement. 'Your car brakes were cut, isn't that reason enough?'

She wrinkles her nose, then gives me a smile. 'Sorry, I'm not used to all this cloak and dagger stuff. I still can't believe it wasn't an accident.'

'Elias is worried too, it's not just me, Helen. Anyway, I won't be long, I have to go shopping.'

FIFTEEN MINUTES LATER, I'm back at the hotel with bags overflowing with stuff for both of us. She's not going to like it but hey, it's better than staying in here all day.

The elevator's packed so I take the stairs and arrive out of breath.

'What did you get?' she calls as soon as I come in.

I pull out her wig, I couldn't resist buying it.

Her face falls. 'I'm not wearing that!'

I can't help but smile. 'Oh, come on Helen, it's not that bad.'

I put on the short blond punk wig, wrap a silver scarf around my neck and strike a pose - that gets her laughing.

'And there's more Helen, look at this.'

I give a theatrical flick of my hand and pull out a trendy looking purple outfit.

She shakes her head in dismay. 'I can't wear that, it's awful!'

'If you want to go out you have to wear a disguise, that's all I could find.' I hold it up to me a give her a twirl. 'You'll look good in this Helen.'

She can't help but laugh. 'Okay, at least no one will recognize me. What did you get?'

I do a drum roll then hold up a long gray dress and a black wig.

She bursts out laughing.

At least I've made her laugh if nothing else.

THE RUSH HOUR traffic isn't too bad, so it doesn't take long to reach the teleferique, unfortunately we forgot about the steps we have to climb to get into the cable car, Helen will never make it.

Back in the car Elias chats to Helen, I'm in the back seat, holding on to the top of his seat as the car speeds up the mountain.

It feels weird being back, especially after what happened to Dev, I know I'm in disguise, but I can't help but think people will still know it's me under this wig.

When we arrive at the casino a few of the blackjack tables are busy, there aren't so many on roulette.

Suddenly I see Theo, Helen's husband, he's at the roulette table, his back is towards us but his arm is around a woman.

Grabbing Helen's arm, I gently steer her over to the elevator where Elias is waiting.

'What's the hurry, Beth?'

I grunt. 'Elias is waiting...'

She stops dead in her tracks, turns around and sees Theo and the woman.

The next minute she pulls out her phone and takes a photo of them.

I give her a tug. 'Come on let's go upstairs.'

Just as I turn, I notice the woman Theo is with staring directly at us. She has a strange look on her face. Theo on the other hand is so engrossed in finding out if his bet has won that he hasn't seen us.

Elias touches my arm. 'Is everything okay?'

'Helen's husband's over there,' I mutter, through clenched teeth. 'He's at the roulette table with a woman.'

Elias shakes his head and turns to leave. 'Let's go to Faliron, it's not far, it's much nicer than here, there's a seafood restaurant by the marina.'

Helen just walks over and presses the elevator button. 'No, let's stay here.'

She turns, beckons us over and winks at me. 'I'm glad you made me wear this outfit, Beth.'

Helen won't back down, so we go to the restaurant and find a table with a good view of Athens. We're sitting at the same table where Helen and I sat just a few days ago, it's not so long ago and yet so much has happened.

The waiter arrives with the drinks - sparkling water for Helen and beer for Elias and me. They both order fish and green beans with Greek salad and chips. I order *Imam Bayildi* - aubergine stuffed with onions, garlic and tomatoes. I like it chilled straight from the fridge, but it will probably be lukewarm from one of their serving trays.

While we're waiting Elias talks about his childhood days in Athens and for a while we forget about Helen's husband. The restaurant starts getting busy, the atmosphere's good and I'm reminded of happier times. I used to come here with my ex Alex, we'd have lunch then stroll around the grounds enjoying the mountain air before returning to Athens.

I look over at Helen, she's enjoying herself and looks radiant compared to a few days ago. She catches me watching her and smiles. 'My food's delicious, how is yours, Beth?'

'Great, it's just as I like it. Not too much oil and the chips are good.'

Elias pushes more chips on his fork, pops them into his mouth and nods in agreement. Helen was right about coming here, it's all very relaxing.

'Can you order me a Greek coffee, metreo?' she suddenly asks, getting up. 'I need the loo.'

I stuff the last mouthful of aubergine in my mouth and get up quickly.

She holds her hand up. 'No, finish your meal, Beth.'

'I've finished.' I turn to Elias. 'Coffee metreo for me also, please Elias.'

He nods and carries on eating, I walk with Helen to the bathroom. I'm terrified she might feel weak or collapse, so she has no choice.

Five minutes later, we're back.

A few minutes later our coffee arrives, then Elias starts talking about Dev. I'm worried he might mention what happened in the casino the other night, so just in case, I give him a nudge him with my foot.

'How long is it since Dev had a holiday?' I ask.

Elias looks puzzled for a minute, then the penny drops. 'I really don't know, he always seems to be working. A few months ago, I asked him if he would like to come with me to Crete. I was visiting relatives in Chania and thought he'd enjoy a break, but he declined, said he had too much work.'

'Well, I hope he doesn't take a break now, or we'll really be in the shit,' Helen mutters. She drains her coffee and looks at Elias and me. 'Shall we go back to the hotel soon?'

'Of course.' Elias gets up and beckons to the waiter.

'No, it's paid,' I mutter.

He shakes his head. 'Next time it's on me. Now you must excuse me for a few minutes.'

Ten minutes later we're passing through the casino, I can see Helen's husband Theo at the cash desk, he's cashing in his chips, but where is the woman he was with?

As we near the car park I remember the CCTV - did Elias ask the police about it just now when he left the table? I sidle up close beside him. 'Did you find out anything about the CCTV?'

Helen looks at me in surprise. 'What CCTV?'

A piercing scream suddenly fills the air - we stop dead in our tracks.

What the hell was that?

I turn and see the woman Theo was with, she's right behind us, she's staring at Helen - there's a wild look on her face.

Suddenly she leaps forward and pushes Helen to the ground. She's just about to kick her in the head - I run over and kick her leg - she screams and falls down.

Elias runs over, drags Helen away from the woman. The woman turns and with a scream leaps on me and starts punching me.

Someone shouts for her to stop, then she's being pulled off me - she stands staring at me with pure hatred in her eyes, then she turns and runs. I chase after her.

Elias runs after me. 'Leave her,' he says, pulling me back to where Helen's standing. 'Let the police deal with her.'

People are on their phones, taking photos and filming us.

'Maniac!' I shout to the retreating figure. 'She's a bloody nutter.'

Elias grunts. 'Yes, she is crazy.'

I yank myself free from him and watch as the Mont Parnes security officers charge out of the foyer in pursuit of the woman.

'What about Theo?' I ask, turning to Helen. 'Have you seen him?'

'Who cares where he is?' Helen replies strangely calm after what's just happened. 'He's probably with that woman, driving back to Athens.'

Then she gleefully pulls out her phone and waves it at us. 'I have a photo of them, shall we give it to security?'

'Of course.' Elias grabs her phone and runs after the security officers.

A few minutes later he returns. 'I had to tell them where you're staying, Beth, they'll probably come and see you, so be prepared.'

I'm just about to say they already know my address, but stop myself, Helen still doesn't know about Dev and I'm not about to tell her.

I glance over and notice she's on her phone, I'm amazed at how well she's taking it. 'Who are you calling , Helen?'

'Dev, he's meeting us back at the hotel.'

'What! But he's supposed to be resting.'

She looks at me in surprise. 'Why, is he ill?'

I let out a groan. 'I think he was taking today off work, but don't worry.'

She smiles, but I know she doesn't believe me.

Nobody speaks on the way back, Helen looks tired, Elias is deep in thought.

As we reach the hotel, Elias's phone rings, we get out of the car and wait for him to finish his call.

A few minutes later he gets out of his car and walks over to us, he has that worried look on his face. 'You must be very careful, go straight to your room and lock the door, Dev will soon be here.'

23

BETH & HELEN
Plaka Hotel

I'S JUST GONE 4.00 in the afternoon, Helen's sitting on the balcony deep in thought, I'm pacing around the room then stop.

'Are you hungry?' I ask, walking onto the balcony. 'I can get something from room service if you like.'

She nods. 'A Greek coffee and a cake would be nice.'

She follows me inside, switches on the TV and laughs. 'Look Beth, there's an old film with the dialogue in English and Greek subtitles, shall we watch it?'

'No, I have to do something, but you watch it.'

She plonks herself down on her bed and starts watching the film, I go to my room and call reception on the hotel phone.

'They'll be up in a few minutes, with your coffee and cake,' I call.

She grunts.

'Are you falling asleep?' I shout.

'No, I'm watching the film,' she groans.

She sounds very sleepy, maybe it's good if she does fall asleep. I start flicking through my emails, I want to have another look at the photos of the men in the casino.

I stand staring at them wondering who they are. They look as if they could be wearing disguises just like Helen and I did - hats, sunglasses, spectacles, beards - who wears dark glasses to a casino? What's the point of even looking at them?

A few minutes later there's a light knock on the door, it must be room service. I glance over at Helen, she's fallen asleep.

I run to open the door, I don't want them to wake her. But when I open the door nobody's there.

Popping my head around the door I shout. 'Anyone there?'

No reply.

What a cheek! Who knocks on a hotel door then disappears? As I turn to go back inside, something hard hits my head.

'What the...'

I turn to see who it is - then everything goes black.

'ARE YOU OKAY?'

I hear a voice, it seems far away.

'What happened?' I mumble, trying to sit up, but I can't. I open my eyes and see a waiter peering at me. My head hurts, I feel sick.

'Someone hit you,' he blurts out. 'I tried to stop her, but she ran away.'

There's a tray of coffee and cakes on the floor next to me, I try to get up, he stops me.

'Don't move, the ambulance will be here soon.'

'I'm okay, what about Helen?'

'Don't worry, I called the police, your friend is safe, she's sleeping.'

Another member of the hotel staff suddenly arrives. 'The police are here,' he calls, excitedly.

A few minutes later the doors of the elevator open, a paramedic gets out. He comes over, examines me then gently lifts me into the chair he brought with him.

'Where are you taking me?'

'Hospital,' he mutters.

'Wait!'

I turn and look at the waiter. 'Can you get my phone for me, it's in my room, probably on my bed.'

He nods and runs into my room.

A few seconds later he appears waving my phone. 'I have your phone.'

The paramedic rolls his eyes, I thank the waiter, then I'm wheeled into the elevator, clutching my phone.

AFTER HAVING AN X-RAY, I'm wheeled to another room, the nurse says she'll be back in a minute.

I try to get up but still feel dizzy and sit holding my head.

'Drink this.'

I look up. It's Dev. He places a polystyrene cup of tea in my hands.

'Drink this it will help.'

'What are you doing here?' I mumble, swallowing the tea.

'I went to your hotel, I saw the commotion, the manager told me you were here.'

'It was the woman from the casino, wasn't it?'

He just stands looking at me with that serious look on his face.

'Don't worry Dev, I'm okay, and thanks for the tea.' I don't take sugar, but it's just what I need. I start thinking about the woman who attacked us outside the casino, it must be the same woman who did this, who else would do this. I take another sip of tea and look at Dev. Helen said he'd arranged for Theo to be followed, so maybe he knows who this woman is?

'You were lucky,' Dev says, pulling up a chair next to me. 'If the waiter hadn't arrived when he did.'

A nurse suddenly appears. 'I have good news the x-ray is okay.'

She has a plastic cup of water and a couple of large white tablets which she puts in my hand.

'Take these, they will help, they are very strong. Then you go home and rest.'

'Thanks.'

I gulp them down and she leaves.

'Elias stopped me running after her...' I mutter. 'I shouldn't have listened to him.'

Dev frowns.

'Have the police caught her yet?'

He stands staring at me, saying nothing.

'What about a little compassion?' I mutter. 'I'm the one who just got hit over the head.'

He raises an eyebrow but says nothing.

'What's wrong with you?'

He gives me a funny look.

'What about Theo, have the police spoken to him yet?'

I try to get out of the chair, he holds onto me to stop me from falling.

I sit down again, I feel so angry.

'Maybe Theo put that woman up to it? I mean, just think about it. If Helen's killed who inherits? We're attacked in broad daylight and then she tries to kill me. Maybe Theo got that woman to cut the brakes of Helen's car, she's crazy enough, it didn't work and...'

Dev's looking at me strangely, does he know who did it?

'I told you this was going to get nasty,' he snaps.

I try to get up but fall back onto the chair again. 'If you lot got your act together, none of this would've happened.'

He takes my empty cup, throws it in the bin, looks at me for a minute, then turns and walks out of the room.

A few minutes later my phone rings. Thinking it's Dev I pick it up. 'Yes?'

'Is that Beth - Beth Papadakis?'

'Yes, who is it?'

'David, I'm a friend of Helen's, I just tried calling her, but she isn't answering...'

Who the hell is David?

'Sorry, I should explain,' he says quickly. 'I'm from Spain, I'm an old friend of hers, I read about the car crash and called her office, Tula said she's at the hotel, but she doesn't answer her phone.'

I don't say anything, he carries on.

'The hotel gave me your number.' He stops and hesitates for a minute. 'They said a woman attacked you.'

'Helen's okay,' I reply. 'I'm sorry David, but now is not a good time, I'll call you tomorrow?'

I'm just saving his number when I see Elias rushing through the door. He immediately spots me and comes over.

'Dev called me, he told me what happened. How are you?'

'I'm okay. I just have a bit of a headache.'

He comes over, holds my hand, as if to comfort me. 'Have you spoken to the doctor?' His eyes look puffy, he probably hasn't slept much. He's always running around Athens in search of the latest news and now Dev gets him to come and see me.

'Don't worry Elias, the x-rays are okay, they gave me some pills which are really good.'

As if to confirm this I get up and this time I don't fall back in my chair.

'I think Dev is right,' he murmurs, a worried look on his face.

I look at him in surprise. 'What do you mean?'

He stands watching me, frowning. 'Beth, I think it would be better for you and Helen to go to London until this is cleared up, you were lucky this time, but next time...'

I've grown fond of Elias and hate to see him looking so worried. I give his hand a quick squeeze and smile. 'Don't worry, I'll make sure Helen's safe, no more Mont Parnes for a while.'

He just stands staring at me. 'But how can you make sure Helen's safe?'

I look at him, can I trust him?

'I'm not sure, Elias, but I have an idea. I just received a call from a friend of Helen's, he heard about her accident, he called the hotel, but she didn't answer. Then he spoke to reception and they said she was asleep, they told him what happened and gave him my number.'

'But who is this man?' he snorts, looking surprised. 'Do you know him? And how can he help you?'

'I'm not sure yet, I said I'd call him tomorrow.'

Elias sits mulling this over, looking more worried than ever.

'Where does he live, in London?'

'No, Spain, I'll find out more when I see him. Now I must call Helen, let her know about her friend.'

After a few rings she picks up. 'Helen, it's me. A friend of yours just called me. He tried calling you, but you must have been asleep.'

'Oh, Beth! Thank God it's you,' she exclaims, sounding relieved. 'I've been so worried, how are you?'

'I'm okay, I'll be back soon. Listen, the guy who called me, his name is David, he's here from Spain. Do you know him?'

'Yes, of course, I haven't seen him for months. How on earth did he get your number?'

'The hotel gave it to him. You were asleep and he was worried about you.'

As soon as I finish talking to Helen, Elias comes over.

'I'll drop you off at your hotel now Beth, shall I get a chair to wheel you outside?'

'I'm staying here for a while, Elias. Go home and get some sleep, you look tired.'

His eyebrows shoot up making him look like a startled rabbit. 'I'm not leaving you to go home alone.'

I appreciate his concern, I really do, but I need to think.

'I'll sit in reception for a while, sort my head out.'

'No, I must take you back to your hotel, I refuse to leave you here on your own.'

I give him a hug. 'Don't worry so much, I'm okay. I just want to be alone for a while. I'll take a cab back and have an early night.'

After making me promise to get a cab back to the hotel, Elias has no choice but to leave.

I sit drinking tea and thinking. Helen's husband Theo must know where the woman who attacked us lives. I try calling him at their home number. No reply!

I still feel a bit weak, so I decide to get a sandwich from the hospital café.

With another cup of tea and a cheese sandwich I go to the far side of the café, find an empty table, take a sip of tea, then give Theo a call - still no reply.

My phone rings. It's Helen.

'Elias just called. He said you're still at the hospital, are you okay?'

'I'm fine, I told him not to worry! I'll be back soon.'

'Beth, I am worried. Shall I call Dev to come and get you?'

'No, don't call Dev, I feel a lot better, the pills the nurse gave me must be working. I'm just having a cup of tea, then I'll get a cab back to the hotel.'

'Okay, but I can easily get a cab, we can come back together, I don't want you to be alone.'

'No, really, I'm fine, I'll see you soon.'

After finishing my sandwich, I gulp down the rest of my tea, go to the ladies, wash my face, put on some lipstick and leave the hospital, now to find a cab.

As soon as I'm outside the fresh air seems to wake me up. I look around for a cab - there are two with their lights on.

I'm just about to ask one of them to take me to the hotel, then change my mind.

'The *Up All Night Club* in downtown Athens, it's just off Omonia Square.'

He nods, I get in the back of the cab.

Let's see what Helen's husband Theo has to say for himself.

24

BETH & THEO

Up All Night Club
8.15 pm

The driver drops me off in a darkened side street near Omonia Square in downtown Athens. Above the entrance to the *Up All Night Club* is the silhouette of a naked woman sitting in a glass, her long legs are crossed, she's smoking a cigarette, the place looks downright seedy.

Athens is well known for its hedonistic nightlife and relaxed drinking laws, glamorous bars and nightclubs in the city and near the beach. There are bars tucked away in tiny side streets which offer some of the best Rembetika music in Athens, but this club I'm looking at right now is not one of them.

Theo never invited Helen to his club and in the end she couldn't care less if she went or not. He said it was a business, a drinking club for men and he didn't want his beautiful wife to be in such a place. By the looks of the place I get the feeling he's right. Taking a deep breath, I enter the club.

A tall heavy-set man with a face like a boxer looks me up and down. Wrapping my thick cardigan tightly around me, I nod, force a smile to my face, walk past him and over to reception. I'm not dressed for clubbing and he knows it. Thick woolly blue cardigan, three quarter length beige trousers and a pair of black pumps are not for this type of place.

The girl at reception has an amused look on her face. 'Yes, can I help,' she asks, looking me up and down. Her accent's Eastern European, she's heavily made-up, charcoal lined eyes, false eyelashes, bright red lipstick and short spiky black hair. 'Do you have an appointment with someone?'

I have an urge to wipe that smug look off her face, but of course I don't.

'I don't have an appointment, I just want to speak to Mr Panikos.' On closer inspection I'm amazed how young she is, underneath the heavy make-up, she can't be more than sixteen years of age.

A sly smile suddenly appears on her pretty round face and she gives me a knowing look. 'But of course, please take a seat, I will tell him you are here. What is your name?'

'Beth,' I reply, feeling slightly uncomfortable, 'Beth Papadakis.'

She lowers her head and speaks in a hushed voice into a phone. The minutes pass, I can tell she's holding on because she's no longer speaking, maybe he's not here? I turn to leave.

'Mr Panikos will see you now,' she says, raising her head

and pointing to a door. 'Go through that door, the one on the right, then go straight through, he's waiting for you.'

Following her directions, I walk over to the door and push it open. The room is luxuriously furnished and dimly lit. I pass through an alcove into an even darker room where there are lots of round tables, set around a stage. It's like a cabaret club, but where is the singer? The air is heavy with the scent of perfume - on my right is a well-stocked bar where men sit drinking. A girl sporting a thong with tiny tassles and a long black plait, tied to the top of her head, walks over to me.

'Can I help?' she asks in a sickly sweet voice.

'Yes, I've come to see Mr Panikos.'

'Follow me.' She turns and leads me round the side of the room and into another room. We pass more alcoves - too dark to see inside as no lights are on. Some even have curtains drawn - maybe for those not wanting to be recognized?

After a while my eyes adjust to the dark - Theo's sitting at a dimly lit table in one of the alcoves, the curtain is half drawn and in front of him is a young well-rounded girl with short blond hair, gyrating around a pole, totally naked.

I know nightclubs are sometimes sleazy, but this is Helen's husband.

The girl who brought me here goes over to him, bends down and talks to him. His hand is in between her legs, I turn to leave.

'Beth, what a surprise, how nice to see you.'

I swing round, he has a wide smile on his face. Without showing any sign of embarrassment, he points to the chair next to him. Then he beckons to the waitress. 'Bring some champagne.'

'I came here to talk,' I say, amazed that he expects me to sit with him here. 'Is there somewhere we can go?'

'Of course.' He turns and claps his hands as if to dismiss the girl who's still gyrating on the pole. She bends, picks up her tiny thong from the stage and runs from the room.

'We will go to the bar. What will you drink?'

'Nothing,' I reply, watching him closely. He's behaving as if nothing's wrong, as if he does this every day. What about Helen? What about the casino - the hotel - the woman he was with who tried to kill us?

He turns to the bar, I follow, glad to get out of the dimly lit room.

'Two coffees,' he calls as we pass the bar and head over to one of the tables. He sits on a red velvet chair and pats the chair next to him. Does he really think I'm going to sit next to him?

'Is there a toilet in here?' I ask, looking around.

'Just behind you,' he replies, pointing to a room with the figure of a naked woman embossed in gold on the door.

The toilet is large, dimly lit with bottles of perfume and other things women might need. There are about six cubicles lining the room. I go into one and check for CCTV and bugging. There's nothing here so I perch on the closed seat and call Dev. No reply so I send him a text saying I'm at the *Up All Night Club*, just off Omonia Square, with Helen's husband and to call me asap.

Taking a deep breath, I open the door. Theo is leaning back in his chair, legs crossed, his black eyes glint as he watches me walk towards him. A shiver runs down my spine, I hug my woolly cardigan around me, walk around the table and sit on the edge of the red velvet chair opposite him. I always had a bad feeling about him, and I was right.

He's watching me with an amused look on his face, his lips curl into a smile, but it looks more like a sneer.

Leaning forward I look directly into his eyes. 'Your girl-friend attacked Helen outside the casino today, then she tried to kill me in my hotel.'

He sits watching me his black eyes dead, like pools of darkness. Gone is the smile. His lips are set in a thin line as he drums his slim fingers impatiently on the top of the table. Raising his eyebrows he slowly shakes his head, as if in disbelief. 'I have no idea what you are talking about, I have no girl-friend.'

'Oh, cut the crap Theo, you're talking to me. I know exactly what you've been up to, for once in your life be honest, the police have a photo of you with her, and they also have CCTV footage, so don't deny you were with her.'

'How dare you,' he hisses, thumping the table with his fist.

Those at nearby tables turn and stare, this infuriates him even more.

Trembling with rage he stands and leans forward, I instantly lean back, his breath stinks of whisky. 'I have friends, friends in high places, so be careful, be very careful you stupid woman.'

I want to laugh, he's so pathetic. 'What's the name of the woman you were with at the casino?' I ask, glaring back at him. He stares at me for a minute then grabs my arm and pushes me out of the room.

'Take your hands off me,' I yell, trying to push him away, but he's stronger than he looks.

I'm frog-marched out of the room then down a small corridor into a luxuriously decorated room. It looks like an office - probably his with soft furnishings, a chandelier in the centre of the ceiling and low lights at the sides.

'Now you stupid bitch, I...'

Then he stops and starts to chuckle. His breathing is heavy, he looks drunk. His eyes are on my body, then with a quick flick of his wrist he hauls me across his desk and begins pulling at my trousers.

'You bastard,' I scream, trying to kick him in the balls. But I can't reach him. He's pulling my trousers off. Then with all his weight on me, he puts one of his hands inside my pants and pulls them down. He's squeezing my butt and mumbling disgusting words in Greek. His breath quickens as he slips his hand between my legs.

In a desperate attempt to get some leverage, I pull my body upwards as far as I can away from him. He laughs and takes his weight off me and flicks me over. 'You have a fat little ass which I am going to enjoy spanking, but first...'

With all the strength I can muster, I pull up my knee and kick him in the face. He screams with pain and clutches his face. Another kick, this time to his groin sends him flying across the room. He lays stunned, blood pouring from his nose.

'That'll teach you,' I hiss. My pants and trousers are on the floor where he threw them, I quickly pull them on, I must get out of here fast.

He starts shouting in Greek.

If I don't do something quick, he'll call for his henchmen, then God help me.

Avoiding his outstretched hand, I stand over him and kick him.

He screams in pain and hunches over.

Shaking with fury, I quickly leave the room. I walk down the corridor, until I can see the club entrance. Nobody sees me. The girl's busy talking to the heavy-set man, so I very quietly slip out of the front door, then run as fast as I can down the street. I must get away I must hide, but where? He'll have his strong men out looking for me.

A car draws up beside me, I run faster, I can't breathe, my chest hurts. How can he have alerted his men so quickly?

I spot a bar. I'm just about to go charging in when I hear a familiar voice.

'Beth! Stop. It's me, Dev.'

Dev!

I turn and see him getting out of his car then he runs towards me.

'What's wrong,' he shouts, grabbing my arm and pushing me into the front seat of his car. 'What happened? Why did you go to that club?'

'First, let's get out of here,' I say, staring at the street ahead.

He puts the car into gear and ten minutes later we arrive at my hotel.

'Well, are you going to tell me what happened?' he asks, staring ahead, not looking at me.

I relay the events of the past hour and feel him stiffen when it comes to the bit about Theo dragging me into his office.

A few minutes pass then he turns and looks at me.

'How's your head.'

'It's alright, I'm okay.'

'Are you sure?'

I nod.

Without looking at him I slide out of the car.

'I'll call you later,' he says, as I slam the door shut. 'And get some sleep.'

I walk into the hotel, he waits till I'm inside then drives off.

A few seconds later I'm in my room, the adjoining door's open, I can see Helen asleep in bed.

Tiptoeing into the bathroom I turn on the shower.

Ten minutes later, with a towel wrapped around me I grab a couple of miniature brandies from the small fridge, gulp them down and fall into bed.

25

BETH

Plaka Hotel - 7.30 am

THEO IS CHASING me through dark, dank tunnels under the streets of Athens. Then I wake up, the hotel phone is ringing. My face and body are covered in sweat, I sit staring at the phone. Shall I pick it up? Who is it? Maybe it's Dev?

I grab it. 'Yes.'

It's not Dev, it's Theo.

'I've contacted my lawyer and he is contacting the police. I know what you're up to, so expect a visit from them soon.'

'What the hell are you talking about, I should be the one contacting the police, you assaulted me.'

'I did what? You stupid, stupid woman, you came to me, I didn't ask you to come.' He hesitates for a minute then carries on. 'You think you get away with this?'

I'm just about to put the phone down when he says...

'It's very strange, you went back to London and so quick, and you her best friend. You probably paid someone to cut the brakes of her car. You think you are clever, you get her to change her will.' He stops for a second then carries on. 'I heard my wife talking to the lawyer telling him to change benefactor to you. To you…' he shrieks, his voice shakes with rage.

I leap out of bed, knock my leg on the bedside table and scream with pain. 'How dare you,' I hiss. 'You...' Then I remember Helen, she's asleep.

I tiptoe over, close the door then in a low voice say. 'You cut her brakes and when that didn't work, you tried again. That women at the casino, she could have killed her, if I hadn't been there...'

'Idiot, the woman works for me, she is not my girlfriend.' His voice is heavy with disgust. 'She left me in the casino, so I found another girl and took her to my club, we...'

I want to scream, but say nothing.

He starts laughing. 'You stupid woman, I have a video of me with this girl. I show it to the police this morning.' Then he stops laughing. 'Next time we meet I teach you a very good lesson.'

I switch off my phone, go onto the balcony, close the door and call Dev.

'I was going to call you later,' he mutters sleepily. 'How are you?'

'Dev, Theo just called me.'

He's silent for a few seconds. 'I'll be at your hotel in a few minutes.'

As he puts down his phone, I'm sure I can hear a woman talking. Well, well, well - I wonder who she is. Did I interrupt something? For some reason I didn't think Dev was seeing anyone.

After a quick shower, I throw on a pair of jeans and a jumper. I make my way to the terrace where breakfast is being served.

A few minutes later I'm sipping a strong black coffee thinking about Theo.

'Good morning!'

Dev sits in the chair opposite me. As always, he looks clean and fresh. I inhale his soft clean fragrance and look at his serious face.

'Why did you go to the club without telling me?' he asks, frowning.

'I was angry, I wanted to have it out with him.'

'The man is getting his lawyer to build a case against you. He's a nasty piece of work and could be very dangerous, you should never have gone there.'

'It's easy to say that now,' I say, peering at him sideways. 'How was I to know what a degenerate he is?'

'So, what did he say?' he asks, slightly impatiently.

'He said I paid someone to cut the brakes on Helen's car, then went back to London so I would have an alibi.'

He gets up, walks over to the bar, gets a coffee and comes back.

'Anything else?'

'He said he heard Helen telling her lawyer to change her will, he said I'm her benefactor. The man's obviously insane, he should be locked up.'

Dev sits staring at his coffee, then picks it up and drinks it. 'Can you think of anyone, other than Theo, who would want to kill Helen?'

'No, I've racked my brain. I have no idea who would want to hurt her.'

I'm missing something but what is it? Then I think of the

CCTV footage in Helen's car park. Dev said someone was standing next to her car, acting suspiciously.

'What about the CCTV footage?' I ask, turning to look at him. 'Have you found out who it was?'

'No, we're working our way through all the mug-shots.'

Suddenly he pushes his chair back and stands up. 'Let me know if you think of anything, and don't go anywhere or do anything until I speak to you. Stay here.'

He gives me a last penetrating look with his blue eyes, then leaves.

I wonder if he does have someone stashed away in his apartment, wherever that may be. I must ask Helen where he lives.

Leaning over the balcony I watch as he walks towards his car. Suddenly he turns and looks up at me, he stays like this for a couple of seconds then gets in his car and drives off.

I have no intention of staying in the hotel and go downstairs.

After walking around Ermou Street and the surrounding area for a while I return to my room, Helen's still asleep.

With my laptop on my knees I make a list of everything I've done from the time I arrived in Athens, to the present.

What am I missing?

I feel on edge I want to do something. I can't stop thinking that I've missed something, but what? Then my phone rings. It's Dev, he doesn't sound happy.

'Theo has reported you, he says you attacked him and accused him of attempted murder.'

'What!'

I stand shaking with rage, I want to... 'He assaulted me, he should be locked up, he's...'

Dev cuts me off sharply. 'He does have friends in high

places, and he knows about Helen's lawyer. What he doesn't know is that we have evidence of his infidelity, and he doesn't know about me.'

'What are you going to do?'

'It's not so bad,' Dev continues, softening his tone. 'We also have friends in high places. They're working right now to get him to drop this case, if they succeed, you must leave Athens for a while.'

I sit holding my phone, thinking how much I loathe Theo.

'Did you hear me?' he snaps.

'Yes, let me know what happens.'

Helen's sitting up in bed, did she hear what I said? I get up and walk over to her. 'I'm making you a coffee you can have it on the balcony with some of those Greek biscuits you like.'

She sits rubbing her eyes then crawls out of bed. 'Okay, I'll just have a quick shower.'

For some reason I feel very alert and focused. What Dev said about Theo made me so angry.

A few minutes later the coffee's ready. Helen's still in the shower so I give her friend David a call, he might be able to help, maybe she can stay with him for a couple of weeks?

'David - it's Beth, Helen's friend.'

'Beth, how lovely to hear from you, I'm just a block away from your hotel.'

'Great, I'll meet you downstairs, I'll be at the entrance.' Now to tell Helen.

I tap on the bathroom door. 'David's coming to see you, I'm meeting him downstairs, then I'll bring him up here.'

The door opens, she looks startled. 'You can't, I'm having a shower!'

'Don't worry. I'll keep him downstairs for a while, don't forget your coffee's on the balcony.

AT THE ENTRANCE to the hotel there's a tall slim man with dark blond hair. Shit. I forgot to ask her what he looks like, but he's the only man here so it must be him.

'David?' I ask, walking over to him.

He swings round and looks at me, a glint of amusement in his dark eyes. 'Yes, you must be Beth.'

I nod. 'Helen's getting ready so shall we have a quick coffee first?'

'Of course, lead the way.'

He follows me into the downstairs café to a table by the window. I glance sideways, taking in his fine Spanish features, blondish brown hair and subtle cologne. We order coffee and sit chatting about Athens.

'So, are you on holiday now?' I ask. 'Or is this a business trip?'

He leans back in his chair and looks at me. 'I was visiting a friend when I read about Helen's accident. We met a few years ago at a travel conference in Athens, we've been friends ever since.'

'Are you still in travel?'

'Yes, travel runs in the family, my parents have a small hotel on the Costa del Sol.'

'How nice,' I murmur, smiling to myself. It couldn't be better, maybe Helen can stay with him for a while.

He grins, leans forward, props his elbows on the table and looks at me with his dark mischievous eyes. 'It sounds nice, but it's hard work. When I finished university, I returned to Spain and helped them, this is where I spend most of my time.'

'So, your parents are Spanish?' Of course, they are - what else can they be - smooth olive skin, lovely dark eyes.

'Actually, I'm half English,' he says, leaning back and watching me. 'My dad's Spanish, my mother's English, what about you?'

'Same as you, but my dad's Greek.'

'I thought there was something Mediterranean about you,' he replies, looking at me closely.

Strange, most people think I look English - blonde hair, green eyes.

I shrug. 'Do you speak Spanish and English?'

He laughs. 'Yes, I went to school in Spain, what about you?'

'My Greek was good when I lived here, but since I've been back in London, I feel I'm losing it.'

'Yes, I know what you mean. I'm going to London tomorrow for a few days, then back to Spain. Are you staying long in Athens?'

That doesn't give me much time to arrange something for Helen.

'I'm not sure, I'm worried about Helen, she needs to relax and get away from here for a few days.'

He sits sipping his coffee, a thoughtful expression on his face. We chat for a few more minutes, then take the elevator upstairs to see Helen.

'Helen, David's here,' I call, opening the door.

She comes into her room from the balcony and smiles.

'David, how are you, it's been a long time since I saw you.'

He walks over and kisses her on both cheeks. 'I'm fine, but what about you, I heard about the accident, how are you?'

I watch them chatting, I'll slip out for a few minutes, give them some time together.

'I'm going to the bakers to get some pastries,' I say, walking to the door. 'I won't be long.'

It's mid-morning, well, just gone eleven when I leave the hotel. The streets are already busy, restaurants are preparing for lunch and some of the corner shops and kiosks are open. I pop into the local bread shop for a bag of pastries.

They're chatting happily on the balcony when I return. 'I hope you're hungry?' I call. 'I bought some cheese pies.'

David quickly clears away the cups so there's room on the table. 'Sounds great!'

'I'll get some plates.' I start rummaging around in the drawers and cupboards, I'm sure we have some somewhere. We have a kettle, tea bags, sachets of Nescafe, a couple of bowls, where are the plates? Then I see them under the serviettes.

'David's going to London,' Helen calls, sounding excited. 'He'll be staying there for a week, he's asked me to go with him, have a sort of holiday. What do you think?'

Now this exceeds my wildest expectations, I feel like a cat who's just found a bowl of cream.

Grabbing a couple of plates, I walk quickly back onto the balcony. 'Sounds great! What a wonderful idea, where will you stay.'

'A friend of my dad's, he has a hotel,' David says. 'There's lots of room so —' He smiles and looks at Helen, she looks so happy.

I just stand staring at him, he carries on talking.

'I always stay there for free, so I'll see if there's a suite vacant. It's close to the park, so good for Helen to relax. It will be just like staying in an apartment, there are two bedrooms, a small kitchen and a small living room, very compact.'

'How lovely,' I say beaming at them both. 'Where's the hotel and when are you going?'

'It's in Park Lane.'

'Wow, you dad's friend must be loaded?'

He laughs. 'Yes, he is.'

David goes inside to call them, then pops his head round the door. 'I'll book an extra flight for you Helen.'

For some reason I feel a twinge of envy. I know it's good for Helen, especially now, isn't that what I wanted? As if reading my mind, David quickly adds.

'You know, the suites are big, there's plenty of room for you Beth. Why don't I leave you two alone for a few minutes? I'll make a few phone calls...'

I laugh. 'There's no reason for you to go inside David, it's a very good idea, Helen needs a break, but I must stay here for a few more days. When I get back to London, I'll come and see you. I live in Bayswater, it's not far from where you'll be staying in London.'

I grab some beers and cokes from our small fridges and place them on the table alongside the pastries I just bought.

David's on his phone sending emails and Helen's face is flushed with excitement.

Within a matter of minutes David jubilantly announces there's a top floor suite vacant for the next ten days, their flight leaves tomorrow evening. Of course Helen's over the moon.

'Fantastic,' I say, smiling at them both. Suddenly I want to go with them. I feel my shoulders slump and my smile fades. Why *am* I staying in Athens? But I know why I'm staying. If I left, I'd never forgive myself. I must find James's killer and there are also the police to deal with.

'I have to speak to Elias,' I say, walking to the door. 'You finish sorting this out, I'll be downstairs if you need me.' Out of the corner of my eye I can see Helen watching me, probably wondering what's so urgent, but she doesn't say anything.

26

ELIAS

LATE AFTERNOON

ELIAS HAS JUST FINISHED WORK, he's been up since 5.00 this morning, its now 5.00 in the afternoon. He feels tired and hungry, he hits the elevator button for the top floor.

Two minutes later he's opening his front door. The spicy aroma of loukanika sausages still clings to the air from breakfast this morning, he'd forgotten to put the air extractor on.

Pulling open the fridge he smiles happily at the bottles of beer in front of him, on the shelf below are sausages, cheese and olives, the inside door contains milk, orange juice and eggs - he sighs and surveys the shelves but doesn't feel hungry.

Popping open a beer he glugs it down quickly, then clutching another beer he saunters into his living room, switches on a few side lamps and opens the French windows onto the balcony.

The hum of traffic and the stunning view of the distant mountains are why he loves his apartment. Kicking off his shoes he collapses into his favourite balcony chair, places his beer on the floor and closes his eyes.

A few minutes later a car hoots and wakes him. He gets to his feet, pads into the living room, sinks down onto the chesterfield couch and stretches out his tired aching legs.

Now where's the remote?

Soon the large TV on the wall springs into action. Sighing with contentment he settles down to watch the news. His eyes are closing, he begins to snore.

Suddenly he's wide awake. The vibration of his phone has roused him.

'*Neh* (yes),' he mumbles.

'Elias, can I come and see you just for ten minutes? I need to talk to you.'

It's Beth, she sounds anxious.

'Of course, you know where I live. It's No 22, top floor – name's on the door – Elias Demetriades.'

'Thanks! See you soon.'

Elias scrambles off the couch and into the kitchen. A quick coffee and something to eat will make him feel better. A couple of old croissants poking out of a bag catch his eye, they'll do until dinner time.

He sits in the kitchen thinking of Beth, munching stale pastries and drinking coffee.

I wonder what's so urgent.

He frowns, drains his mug of coffee then makes a quick visit to the bathroom.

His doorbell rings, zipping up his trousers, he washes his hands.

It must be Beth, she got here fast.

He goes to open the door, but it isn't Beth. Standing in front of him is a tall, slim guy with a black balaclava covering his face. All Elias can see are two black eyes.

The man suddenly springs forward, startling Elias, he takes a step back and gasps. A large blade is coming towards him. He tries desperately to close the door, but the guy's foot is in the way.

Suddenly there's a piercing scream.

Thinking his time has come Elias closes his eyes.

I FEEL bad not telling Helen where I'm going so I give her a quick call, it goes to voicemail, I leave a message saying I'll be back soon.

For a Sunday there's not much traffic, so it doesn't take long to reach Elias's place. Once inside the elevator I hit the button for the top floor. As the doors open I get a weird feeling something's wrong. I glance around, there's a tall guy with something black pulled over his head. Then I notice the door number, it's Elias's place.

Running as softly as I can I grab him around the neck, squeeze as hard as I can and at the same time kick him in the back of the legs.

He falls to the floor, I kick him in the groin, he screams with pain.

'Beth!'

I look up. Elias is staring at me as if I'm from another planet. Then the guy on the ground moves to grab the knife, I give him another kick, quickly push him over so he's face down on the ground. 'Give me your belt Elias, quickly,' I yell.

My phone starts ringing, it doesn't stop. I'm holding the

guy's hands behind him, I've one knee on his back. 'Elias! Help me!'

Elias suddenly snaps out of it, runs over and ties the guy's hands with his belt.

I grab the knife, then answer my phone.

'Where are you?' Dev shouts. 'Helen just called me.'

'I'm at Elias's place. I just stopped him from being killed.'

I hear a short intake of breath. 'I'll be there in ten minutes.'

A gasp from someone watching makes me swing round. The guy wearing the balaclava has broken the belt, Elias is spread-eagled on the ground, the guy's stumbling towards the stairs.

Through the slits of the balaclava I can see the hatred in his eyes as he stares at me, then he opens the door to the stair-well.

'Call the police,' I shout.

A man, probably Elias's neighbor pulls out his phone.

Elias gets up, hits the elevator button. A second later the doors open, he jumps in followed by his neighbour. Fortunately, there are only five floors in this stylish 1960s building, all have huge balconies, draped with heavy white canopies.

I watch as the doors of another elevator on the same floor open, jump inside and hit the ground floor button.

As the doors open, I'm greeted by the sound of running feet and shouting, Elias and his neighbour are in hot pursuit of the hooded attacker.

A police car suddenly skids to a halt outside the apartments and all hell breaks loose.

The guy looks as if he's cornered but he's not giving up, suddenly he leaps onto a balcony and disappears.

There's such a commotion, windows and doors are opening, residents lean over their balconies to see what's happening.

I watch as the guy leaps from one balcony to another, he's obviously in good shape. Is he heading for the top floor?

Jumping in the elevator I hit the button for the penthouse level.

'There he is,' shouts someone as I charge out of the elevator.

I turn and see him, he's right on the edge, preparing to leap to the other block. He must be crazy if he thinks he can make it.

He turns, sees me, sticks his finger up in the air, then goes to jump.

The police suddenly appear and grab him. With much swearing and screaming they wrestle him to the ground, handcuff him and escort him back down the elevator to their car.

Back on the ground floor Elias is gesturing for me to stay away, but I want to see who the hooded attacker is.

The police drag him over to their car.

'Take off his hood, I want to see who he is,' I shout, then I point to Elias and add. 'He tried to kill this man with this knife.'

One of the young police officers runs over and takes the knife from me, the other shrugs and pulls the balaclava from the man's head.

It's the guy from the casino, the one who was wearing the owlish looking glasses, even without them I'd know it's him.

He's just about to say something but the police stop him, shove him in the car and drive off.

I look over at Elias, he's talking to Dev who just arrived.

Both are in deep conversation, Elias is obviously telling him what happened. Dev turns and gives me one of his strange looks.

'Who was it?' he shouts.

'Didn't you see?' I ask, walking over to them. 'It was the guy from the casino. He didn't have his glasses on, but I'd know him anywhere.'

We walk to the elevator, press the top floor button, the police follow behind in the other elevator.

After giving statements, we're told we must report to the central police station later that day or by the following morning.

As soon as they've left Elias turns to me. 'You were amazing Beth, you saved my life.'

I look at him and smile. 'You'd have done the same for me, wouldn't you?'

He nods and gives me a hug.

We leave Elias chatting to his neighbour and make our way to the elevator.

'Where did you learn to fight like that?' Dev asks, hitting the down button.

'I told you, I can look after myself.'

He gives me another strange look then we walk to his car.

On the way back I take a quick sideways peek at him, he looks so serious.

He turns and catches me watching him and gives me one of his rare smiles. 'Where did you learn to fight like that, Beth?'

'I told you, I took self defence classes.'

27

BETH, HELEN & DAVID

NEXT DAY

ON MY RETURN from the police station I find David in the hotel foyer.

'I heard all about last night,' he says, walking over to me. 'It's a good job you can look after yourself, how are you?'

I shrug. 'Okay, I just signed an official statement about it at the police station.'

He looks at me quizzically for a minute. 'So you're okay?'

'Yeah, I'm okay.'

'Helen brought me up to date on some things, but she hasn't said much about her husband, only that she wants a divorce.'

I nod. 'Have you finished packing?'

He smiles. 'I pack very quickly,' he hesitates, then looks towards the hotel café. 'Are you hungry?'

'Yes, but Helen's still asleep, maybe I should wake her, see if she wants to eat.'

He nods. 'I called her but she didn't answer. It's good if she sleeps, she needs all the rest she can get.'

'Okay, so let's just have a coffee for now.'

We sit at the same table we did the other day - he's ordering our coffees from the waiter - I'm looking at him. It's hard to tell how old he is, he dresses well, probably Armani, his gray suit fits him like a glove - suddenly I realize he's asking me what I want.

'Sorry David, I was miles away - black coffee please - I'll text Helen to let her know you're here.'

A few minutes later she texts me back:

I just she woke up, give me twenty minutes to get ready.

Twenty minutes later Helen's dressed and waiting for us.

'Let's go to Edem restaurant to eat,' she says, looking at me. 'I know Beth likes it there, it's right on the beach and the food is good.'

'But it might be a bit cold by the sea, Helen?'

She rolls her eyes and laughs. 'It's a lovely day, how can I catch cold?'

David looks at me then at Helen. She links arms with him and laughs. 'Come on, I'm fine, you'll love it there.'

'Where is it?' David asks.

'It's in Faliron,' I reply, following them into the elevator. 'It's the nearest beach resort to Athens.'

We walk to David's car, he clicks his key fob and we all pile in.

'I could do with a bit of fresh sea air,' he says, 'Is it near the famous Alimou Marina in Kalamaki where the sailboat charters are based?'

'Yes,' Helen replies, buckling up her safety belt. She's in the front with him, I'm in the back.

Soon we're parking in a side-street not far from the beach. Sliding out of the car I turn to David and start telling him where everything is.

'The restaurant's over there on the beach and the tram stop's over there...'

Helen laughs, and hugs me. 'You should get an apartment here, then you won't have an excuse not to come to Athens.'

My phone rings, it's Dev.

'Helen, can you grab a table with a sea view and order me something?'

She nods, I answer my phone.

'We need to talk - urgently!'

'Why, what's happened?'

'I can't talk over the phone, where are you?'

'I'm in Faliron, with Helen and David.'

He doesn't reply, so I carry on.

'They're flying to London tonight, they have to be at the airport at 6.00 pm, their flight leaves at 8.10 pm'

'Who is David?'

'He's an old friend of Helen's, it all happened so quickly.'

I can tell he's surprised because he doesn't say anything. I stand looking at the sea - although it's February it feels more like April, people are having a paddle, another is getting ready for a swim. I shiver slightly, the sea won't be very warm now...

'I'll be at the airport at 7.00, I'll call you when I'm there.'

I'm just about to tell him not to worry I can take the bus, but he's gone.

Helen and David are stuffing themselves with calamari and chips when I reach our table. She takes a serviette off a bowl of food and looks at me. 'Sorry Beth, but this is the only thing that you can eat, there's not much for vegetarians and vegans, it's a vegetable risotto.'

'It looks lovely, thanks Helen.'

We start talking about London, then Helen starts talking about the clothes she'll need to take with her.

'Beth, can you go to my house and get me some clothes, I don't want to see Theo, he's always been nice to you.'

I raise my eyebrows. She wouldn't say that if she knew what her Theo did to me, but she doesn't and I'm not going to tell her. But the thought of going into their house... if he catches me... Then I think of my Glock, it's still locked away in a chest of drawers in our apartment. Do I have time to get it? I can wait till Alex has gone to work and...

'Here you are,' Helen says, breaking into my thoughts. 'It's a list of things I need...' She stops and looks at me. 'Are you alright is something wrong?'

'No, I'm fine.'

She gives me a funny look, I can never fool Helen, she knows me to well.

'I don't think he'll be there Beth, if that's what's bothering you. If he is, just say you're picking up some clothes for me. We'll be in the car outside if you need us.'

What can I say? Shall I tell David? He can come with me but then she'll be left alone in the car.

I shrug. 'Write down exactly where they are and don't forget to text me if you see him coming.'

I'm trying to remember the layout of Helen's house. If there's a problem with Theo, will David come and help? Shall I tell him what happened?

After writing down exactly where her clothes are in the spare bedroom where she now sleeps, she hands me the list.

'It's getting a bit chilly, let's collect my clothes and go back to the hotel, I still have to pack.'

We leave the restaurant and pile back into David's car. Helen's in the front with him, I'm in the back.

As we drive to Helen's house in Kolonaki, I ask her to call the house phone to see if Theo's there.

'No reply, he's not there.'

She turns to look at me. 'Don't worry Beth, we'll be outside if you need us.'

Ten minutes later we pull up outside her house, his car isn't there but that doesn't mean anything, maybe it's in the car park?

'Go on Beth, what are you waiting for,' Helen asks, giving me a nudge.

'Alright, but don't forget to let me know if his car pulls up.'

She laughs. 'Don't worry, now go.'

I get out of the car and quickly run to the front door, I ring the bell and wait. No answer, I try it again, still no answer. I can see Helen gesticulating for me to go inside. I insert the key and gently open the door. Once inside I stand still and listen. The only sound is my heart beating. My mouth's dry, I swallow and quickly creep into the living room. Nobody's there…

I make my way up the stairs to one of the guest bedrooms where Helen sleeps, that's where she said her clothes are. I slowly open the drawers and shove her clothes in a bag. I'm nearly finished when I hear something. I freeze. It sounds like creaking floorboards. It must be him, but where is he? I didn't hear him come in and there's no warning text from Helen, she's supposed to text me. Did he climb in through the French windows in the living room downstairs? Shit, I've got to get out of here.

Creeping over to the window I peer out, I can see Helen in the car below. Then I hear a loud moaning noise. Clutching hold of the bag, I creep back into the guest bedroom then tip toe over to the stairs. The moaning noise is louder, it's coming from Helen's bedroom. The door's partly open, it's Theo. He's totally naked. Oh God, does he never stop? Is this all he thinks of? They must have been in the bedroom when I arrived and not heard me.

Shuddering at the thought of what he did to me, I run down the stairs, through the living room and out of the house.

David's holding the back door of the car open. 'What's wrong?' he asks, staring at me. 'You look flushed, was anyone in there?'

'No,' I reply, slamming the car door. 'Let's go!'

I can see Helen's worried face in the overhead mirror.

'Come on David! What are you waiting for?' I yell, but he's staring at the house, I follow his eyes, a curtain moves in the front bedroom.

With a squeal of tires, the car speeds forward, away from Kolonaki Square back to our hotel.

It's late when we arrive at our hotel, Helen grabs the bag of clothes and heads towards the elevator. I glance over at David, I know he saw the curtain move, but he says nothing.

Helen stares at the bag of clothes on her bed, grabs a pair of jeans and a thick jumper and begins to get dressed.

I hold out the long sleeved black thermal vest I found in her drawer. 'Put this on you'll need it in London.'

She looks at me wearily. 'What would I do without you, Beth?'

'You'd manage perfectly well,' I reply, winking. She knows she must take it easy, which reminds me, I must make sure David's aware of this. Long walks in the park in February in London are not what Helen needs.

Eventually we make it to the airport with just a few minutes to spare. David drops off his hired car, then they go through customs. I suddenly wish I was going with them, I wonder where Dev is, maybe he's not coming?

After they've gone through, I stand at the entrance to the airport breathing in the night air. Shall I get a cab or take the bus back to Syntagma?

Then I see Dev hurrying towards me.

28

DEV & BETH

HE LOOKS TIRED, his face is serious, my heart sinks.

'What's so urgent?' I ask, as soon as he's near me.

'Not now,' he answers, gently steering me to the car park. 'I'll tell you later.'

We drive in silence. 'So what's so urgent, Dev?'

He glances over at me. 'Don't be so impatient.'

I shrug. He obviously doesn't want to tell me now so I close my eyes and start to nod off.

Dev taps me on the arm. 'Wake up, we're here.'

'But I thought you were taking me back to my hotel?' I say, sitting up and looking at him. 'Where are we?'

He leans over and opens the door, I slide out.

We're outside a small bar next to the sea. Dev puts his arm around my shoulder and we walk inside. It's not very busy so we have our choice of where to sit. The waiter takes us to a table tucked away in a corner. I ask for wine, Dev orders a coffee. I sit sipping my wine waiting for him to say something, but he just sits drinking his coffee.

'So, why are we here?' I ask, looking around. 'Are we meeting someone?'

He's got his serious face on and just sits looking at me. Then with a deep sigh he leans forward. 'I brought you here because I want to talk to you, and I know you're not going to like what I say.'

I had a feeling he was going to say something but why bring me here?

'There's too much at stake,' he mutters. 'Your safety comes first. So far, you've been very lucky, but you've made many enemies, you won't stand a chance against them. The police contacted me...'

He sits turning his coffee cup around in his hands.

'And?' I ask, watching him closely.

'I contacted someone, and the charges filed against you by Theo have been dropped.'

'So why are you looking so glum?' I ask, peering at him.

'There's something else,' he sighs deeply. 'You must go back to London.'

'And if I don't?'

'Don't even think about it, Beth,' he snaps reverting to his cold detached other self. 'You need a full-time bodyguard otherwise you'll end up dead or in jail. And that's not something you'd like, is it?'

I sit sipping my wine, ignoring him and look out of the window towards the sea. Helen's on her way to London, she'll be there at 10.00 London time, but it'll be midnight here in Athens. Out of the corner of my eye I can see him staring into his coffee. Why didn't I go with Helen? I'd have had company on the flight and wouldn't have to endure this.

I bought a one-way ticket to come to Athens. It was an emergency.

Rolling the stem of the wine glass between my fingers, I take a deep breath and turn to Dev. He's silently watching me with a strange look on his face. 'Okay, I'll book my ticket tonight - happy?'

He takes an envelope from his jacket pocket and hands it to me. 'You're on the 9.15 tomorrow morning. I'll collect you at 7.00.'

For some reason I'm not surprised, I just nod and take the envelope. 'Who do I pay?'

'It's on us, we...'

I stand up and walk towards the door, he follows.

We drive back to the hotel in silence. Then I'm alone back at the hotel, no Helen, just me. Pulling open the fridge, I grab a miniature bottle of brandy and glug it down, wondering where I went wrong. Then I remember the list I made on my laptop before that dreadful woman attacked me.

My phone rings making me jump. Is it Dev? No, it's Elias.

'Beth, I had to phone. I... I know you are going tomorrow and I want to say that if ever you need anything give me a ring.'

My eyes fill with tears. 'Elias,' I croak, wishing he was here so I could hug him. 'All I want is for you to help me find James's killer. Email me, send me everything you find - photos, articles - whatever, and keep me up to date with that scum bag Theo.'

He laughs and promises he'll do this, wishes me a good journey and I'm alone again, staring at the Acropolis, just like I've done a million times before. There's something hypnotic about it and I know I'll be back soon. I'll text Dev early tomorrow morning, say I woke up early and I'm already at the airport, that way I won't have to see him.

Two more little bottles of brandy and I feel a bit better. I curl up on the bed and close my eyes.

THE SOUND of the phone ringing cuts into my dream, I wake with a start. My mouth's dry, I need a drink.

There's a loud knock at the door, then another. I crawl out of bed and open it.

Dev's staring at me, 'You have to get dressed, quickly,' he mutters. 'I'll be downstairs in the car.'

There's no time for coffee on the terrace as usual, no chatting and gazing at the Acropolis, I bite my lip, this isn't supposed to happen, I shouldn't be going home.

We drive to the airport in silence, he parks the car, takes my luggage from the back seat, I grab it from him and start walking towards departures.

'Look Beth,' he says, walking alongside me. 'It's for your own good.'

Gritting my teeth, I carry on walking. I can feel him watching me, he's making bloody sure I get on the plane.

I go through customs and board the plane. Once we're airborne I order a black coffee and a bar of chocolate. I sit gazing out of the window at the retreating sunshine until the last rays of the sun are gone. Snowy white clouds surround us now, I wish I was still in Athens.

During the four-hour flight I try to calm down. I can't stop thinking about it, I feel empty inside. I doze off for a while and have terrible dreams about being chased up the mountain by a car. I'm in a cab but the driver refuses to go faster, I keep telling him the people in the car behind us want to kill me but he only laughs. I wake up drenched in sweat, the woman in the seat next to me is staring at me.

'Are you okay?' she asks, a worried look on her face.

'Yes,' I mumble, sitting up and reaching for my bottle of water. 'I just had a bad dream.'

29

BETH

LONDON

THE BITTERLY COLD wind greets me as I leave London airport, I cross the road to the Tube, but the thought of getting on a crowded train fills me with dread. I walk back to the airport and take a cab to Bayswater.

The apartment feels cold and empty, there's no Jamie to welcome me as usual, he's staying at Mum's. I turn on the heating, switch on the TV - same old rubbish they always show on daytime TV - I turn it off and go into the kitchen.

Half a bottle of Pinot Noir sits on the table reminding me of my last drink in Athens with Dev. It's tempting to fill a glass, but I need something to eat first, I didn't eat breakfast, I only had that chocolate bar on the plane. There's lots of stuff in the freezer but I really can't be bothered to cook, coffee and crackers will do.

Oblivious to the sound of the rain on the living room window, I sit drinking my coffee and munching crackers. I can't stop thinking about Dev and the events of the past few days. Eventually I fill a glass up to the top with Pinot Noir and sit drinking and listening to the rain. With each gulp I take, I feel a little bit better.

After a while I lay down on the couch, close my eyes and start to drift off.

Then my phone rings. Shall I answer it? No, I turn over and ignore it.

It rings again, this time I grab it.

'Beth, I just heard you were back in London. How are you?'

I yawn. 'Not great, I just fell asleep on the couch.' I sit up wondering who told Helen. 'How are you?'

'I'm okay, it's you I'm worried about.'

'Who told you I was here?'

'I called Dev to find out about the case and he told me.' She hesitates then continues. 'He didn't sound very happy, he's worried about you.'

I sit silently holding the phone.

'Are you still there, Beth?'

'Yes,' I groan. 'Well, he'd better get a move on and solve the bloody case. Think about it Helen, they have all that CCTV footage from outside your place, from the casino, and God knows what else from the bar by the beach, surely the owner of the bar remembers something. And what about the car? Who was driving it? Did they catch it on CCTV? For sure the guy must have been speeding - did they clock him for that?'

I stop to draw breath then carry on. 'And what's the name of the guy who was killed with James? These are all questions nobody's answered, or if they have, they're not telling us.'

I pause. Helen's silent, I'm waiting for her to say something, anything.

'Beth, I know how you feel,' she suddenly blurts out. 'But we have to wait. What else can we do? If they won't tell us, there must be a reason. For Dev to ask you to leave means he knows you're in danger, that's why you're here.'

'Yes, he's probably got someone watching us right now,' I snap. 'They were probably watching us in Athens.' Helen doesn't know there were guards at the hospital and I'm not about to tell her. 'Look Helen, I've got to go. I'll call you later. Say hello to David for me.'

I suddenly feel wide awake. I need a coffee and my laptop.

A few minutes later I'm charging my laptop and making a list.

THINGS I MUST FIND OUT.

Name of the guy who was killed with James. His background - where did he work? Where did he live? Is he married? Did he go to university?

Who are his friends?

CCTV footage from Helen's place.

CCTV footage from the casino - did they find the woman who attacked us?

What about the creep who phoned me at the hotel? Have they found him?

Bar by the beach where James was killed - forensic report?

Bar owner - what does he remember? Any CCTV footage of the car the killer was driving? Maybe he was speeding and was caught on camera?

Reasons Theo wants Helen dead?

Gambles heavily in the casino – check his finances.

He inherits a lot if Helen dies, although he did say she'd changed her will recently so that I would inherit – or rather he screamed this information at me – just thinking about him makes me feel sick.

What *am* I missing? My mind's dried up so I rub my head with the tip of my nails. This usually works but today it doesn't, so I give up.

Now to email Elias, see if he can answer these questions. I put URGENT in the subject line then press send.

It's nearly 5.00 in the afternoon and already dark and freezing cold. February's always a miserable month - the hype of Christmas is long gone and it's the coldest month of the year.

I sit staring out of the window at the rain deciding what to do - I need to walk.

With my puffa jacket zipped up I open the door, I'll buy some bread, do some shopping.

I'm soon walking down Queensway. It's cold and raining so I pull up my hood and run to Tesco's supermarket.

Fifteen minutes later I'm hurrying back home clutching two bags of shopping. Living in the centre of London has its advantages, I'm close to the shops, restaurants, transport and Hyde Park. The one drawback is the rent, and you can forget about buying a place, prices are out of reach for people like me. My rent's always going up, so unless I win the lottery or get a better job.

My phone rings as I'm opening the door to my apartment, I drop the bags of shopping, rummage through my small shoulder bag for my phone, find it then it stops ringing.

It was Elias. I call him back, but it's engaged, maybe he emailed me?

Sure enough, there's one from him.

Hello Beth – I hope you had a good journey. Most of the information you want is highly classified. I have connections but Dev has more sophisticated ways of doing things. Have you asked him? I checked the latest article I wrote on James's accident. The guy who was killed instantly, the one he went to meet, had no ID on him, so the next of kin were never contacted. Forensics must have all the info you need but how to get it? Will keep checking and let you know. Elias

My reply.

Thanks. I asked Dev a couple of times but no luck. If you can ask maybe he'll tell you? Beth

I know Elias feels a sense of obligation to me for saving his life and I feel bad pressing him, but if you don't ask, you don't get.

NOW TO TEXT HELEN.

Helen - did you ever get a print-out of the person on the CCTV footage putting something in the hood of your car? If not ask Dev (I don't want to - I'm sure you understand why), and whilst you're about it, ask him if they've tracked down the woman who tried to kill you. And ask if they found out anything about James's wife. Btw send me the photo you took of the woman in the casino. Beth

Then I remember the shopping bags in the hall.

Five minutes later I'm eating French bread with cheese, tomatoes and olives, I'm also on my second cup of strong black coffee.

Now to get started on my Athens article, my editor needs it by tomorrow, so I must be quick.

By the time I finish it's nearly 8.20 and I'm tired. It's been a long day. I wonder if Helen contacted Dev?

I login to my emails, there's one from Helen, attached is a photo of the woman in the casino with Theo. She also sent the woman's name and address in Athens which she got from Dev, the photo's not very clear, but it'll do.

My reply to Helen.

Have they caught her yet? Beth

Now for a large glass of wine and some pizza of which there are many in the freezer.

Back at my laptop I sip the wine and check for anymore emails.

There's one from Helen and another from Elias. Let's see what Helen has to say.

Have contacted Dev about the woman, will let you know what he says. Are you okay? Call me! Helen

Now the email from Elias.

I went to the bar in Glyfada and had another chat with the waiter, but nothing new. He said everything happened so quickly. He has no idea what the car looked like. I asked Dev if there is any CCTV footage of the car and if it was speeding. He didn't answer, but said he is coming round to see me, so not sure what that means. Elias

If only I'd thought about this a few days ago when I was in Athens, I could've checked it out.

There's a ping from the kitchen informing me my pizza's ready.

I settle down on the sofa with a large glass of wine and half the pizza, turn on the TV, and as usual it's nothing but doom and gloom. My head hurts, I'm tired, I finish eating and turn it off, I'll have a short nap on the sofa, then do some more work.

The sound of my phone ringing wakes me. It's Elias, I quickly sit up.

'Beth, I have some news for you,' he chirps, sounding unusually excited. 'Dev came to see me, he just left.' I can hear him shuffling papers, I hold my breath. 'He's coming to London tomorrow. He's arriving in the morning.'

'What!'

I'm suddenly wide awake. I get off the sofa and start walking around the living room.

'Why is he coming, did he tell you?'

'I'm not sure, but he's sure to call you.'

That means he does know but he doesn't want to tell me.

'Are you still there?' Elias asks.

'Yes, I'm just amazed he's coming to London. Did you find out anything? Like the name of the man who was killed with James?'

There's a pause and I know Elias's thinking whether to tell me or not. He knows something, I'm sure. Will he tell me?

'You must not tell Dev I told you - okay?'

I sigh with relief. 'Yes, of course, Elias, you know I won't.'

'The name of the man James went to see is Fivos - Fivos Demoulakis. I don't think it can help you much, you have probably never heard of him.'

'No, it doesn't ring a bell, but thanks for telling me. I really appreciate it Elias. Talk to you soon.'

I sit nursing the phone, thinking, only a few hours ago Dev dropped me off at the airport, now he's coming here. What happened?

It's getting late and I want to get up early tomorrow. I set the alarm on my phone for 8.00 am, then roll into bed, snuggle under the duvet and close my eyes.

30

BETH

Bayswater
London

I wake up feeling better than I have in a long time. After showering I make breakfast - toast, marmalade and coffee. I sit deep in thought sipping my coffee. The sound of the letter box makes me jump, it must be the postman.

A few minutes later I'm flicking through the mail, there's a letter from the estate agent asking why I haven't replied to the letter they sent a couple of weeks ago. I completely forgot about it, it was about them upping my rent, but I have a contract, they can't do this.

Where's that damn contract?

The top drawer of my desk is where I keep this kind of stuff - bills, divorce papers, contracts, letters and things. I start rummaging through it and a pile of letters fall out on the floor. One has a Greek postmark. The address is written in my ex's handwriting. I sit on the floor going through them, until I find what I'm looking for, I am right, they can't raise my rent.

Grabbing my phone, I call the office. The person I need to speak to, isn't there, so I leave a message for him to call me. Then I phone Jamie.

'Hi Mum, how are you, how was Athens?'

'I'll tell you about it when I see you,' I reply. 'What about you, are you okay?'

'Yeah, I'm okay, Nan's out shopping, she'll be back soon, shall I get her to call you?'

'Yes, but first I want to know what you've been doing while I've been away.'

It's just past lunch time when we finish talking. I look at the heap of papers on the floor next to me. Shall I just throw them all in the bin or shred them?

I start shredding. Two then three at a time, I want it to go faster, maybe I can get more in. I add five, then eight at a time. The bloody thing clogs up and stops. I'm on my knees trying to get them out when a letter on the floor catches my eye, it's from my ex Alex, I thought I'd binned most of them. Something's circled in red, I look closer, written on the envelope is the name Fivos Demoulakis.

Fivos Demoulakis!

A shiver runs down my spine – Elias said this was the name of the man James went to see the night he...

Shit! I get up and pour a drink. I stand staring at the envelope, glugging down the wine.

Then it comes to me, I know who it is. A guy from university was called Fivos Demoulakis, he was a friend of Alex's. Could it be the same man?

For the next few hours I sit shredding letters but the one

from Alex I keep. My phone starts ringing - it's Dev, it's 4.20 in the afternoon.

'Hello Beth, I'm in London!'

Am I supposed to know about this? I forgot to ask Elias. 'What a surprise, where are you?'

'I'm at the Venus Hotel, in Park Lane. Helen asked David if he could get me a deal at their hotel.'

'That's nice,' I reply, wondering why Helen didn't tell me about this.

'Listen Beth, this is very important, can we meet somewhere? I need to talk to you.'

What a change from the last time I saw him. He couldn't wait to get rid of me, now he needs to talk to me. 'I'm not sure,' I reply. 'Can't it wait until tomorrow?'

'I wouldn't ask if it wasn't urgent, would I?' he replies, stiffly. 'But if you can't make it...'

'Well if it's that urgent...'

'Yes, it is,' he snaps.

'Okay,' I mumble, already thinking of the quickest way to get there. 'I can be there in about 30 or 40 minutes, is that okay?'

'Great! I'll be downstairs in the hotel bar.'

31

BETH

Later than afternoon

When I get to the top of Queensway, I can see a 148 bus, it goes to Park Lane so I run to catch it. As the bus makes its way up the Bayswater Road to Marble Arch I sit staring out of the window at Hyde Park, I'm always amazed how lovely it looks, even in winter.

Ten minutes later we're at Marble Arch, the bus turns right into Park Lane, then after a few stops I'm outside the hotel, it only took fifteen minutes, I'm early.

Dev's not in the bar so I find a table near the window and start texting him.

'You got here fast,' Dev says, gently pulling me up by the arm and steering me out into the hotel foyer. 'Let's get out of here. We can talk in the park.'

I stop dead in my tracks, what the hell is he doing? 'Dev, this is London not Athens, it's freezing out there.'

'Come on, a bit of fresh air will do you good. It's not that cold and we can talk while we're walking.'

The next minute, we're dodging cars and buses on Park Lane, just to get to the bloody park, I wouldn't mind but it's shrouded in darkness.

Suddenly he stops. 'You're right, it's freezing, let's go back to the hotel - we can talk in my room.'

Rolling my eyes, I push my freezing cold hands deeper into my pockets but say nothing.

We run across the road to the hotel, take the elevator up to his room, and go inside. It's large and very modern, there's a queen size bed, soft coloured drapes and even a small sofa with two comfortable looking chairs.

He takes off his coat and throws it over a chair. 'It's much warmer in here, I'd forgotten how cold London can be.'

'Yes, it's not like Greece is it.' I slip off my coat, he takes it from me and lays it on the bed.

'When did you arrive in London, Dev?'

'Early this morning, I didn't sleep last night.'

That's strange, Elias said he was going to see him last night, so why didn't he grab a few hours before his flight. Then I remember the woman I heard when I called him the other morning.

'Would you like something to drink?' he asks, walking over to the small mini-bar. 'There's a red from Chile, I think you'll like it - Pinot Noir.'

I nod, wondering why he's so nervy, he's in one of his funny moods, I can see the muscle twitching in his cheek, he seems a bit hyped-up which is unusual. I watch as he searches for a couple of glasses and pours the wine. The last time I saw him he was in a bad mood and I was pissed off at being sent home. Helen assured me he only did it for my safety, but he knows I can take care of myself. Has he forgotten what happened to Elias? If it wasn't for me his friend wouldn't be here. So many terrible things have happened, and I've always coped.

He hands me my glass of wine and gives me another funny look. 'Is it alright?'

'Perfect,' I reply, after taking a sip. I find myself somewhere to sit and look at him. 'Now what did you want to tell me?'

Pulling up a chair next to me he takes a sip of his drink, whilst watching me over the rim. 'The things you mentioned to Elias... we checked them out some time ago. I've been waiting for forensics, that's why it's taken so long. I believe Elias told you about it?'

He places his drink on a small table and watches me intently. I'm just about to say he didn't tell me much, but he carries on talking.

'We now know something about the man who was killed with James.' He gets up, walks over to the fridge, I say nothing. 'He attended university in Athens and studied law.' I watch as he opens two more mini bottles of wine wondering where this is going. 'He worked for some years in a law firm, then as a teacher.'

After topping up our drinks he walks over to the window.

'And yes Beth,' he says, turning and looking at me. 'The killer's car was caught on CCTV footage. We've checked it out and the car's registered to a man in Bulgaria, his name is Stefan Bronowski.' He pauses and looks at me. 'Don't get your hopes up, the car was probably stolen. We also know the two are not connected.'

'What, the murder of James and the attempted murder of Helen?'

He's watching me intently, then sits down in the chair next to me. He's wearing a darker coloured suit than usual which makes him look different. His blue shirt matches the colour of his eyes and is open at the neck.

'Two people are in police custody in Athens, Beth. They've both been charged with attempted murder.'

'If you have two people in custody in Athens, why are you here?'

He doesn't answer, just finishes his wine and walks over to the window again.

What isn't he telling me?

'Have you spoken to Helen? Does she know about this?'

He nods.

'So, who have you arrested? James's wife and the crazy woman from the casino?'

'The woman from the casino is one of them. She's mentally unstable, with a history of assaulting people.'

'She needs a psychiatrist,' I mumble, remembering the look on her face when she attacked Helen.

He grunts in agreement. 'She thinks Theo loves her, that's why she hates Helen.'

'But he screws around with so many women!' With a shudder I remember what happened in his club.

'Yes, but in her mind, she thinks she's the only one, or so she says. Maybe she's just blocked it out, maybe she's in denial.' He shrugs. 'Anyway, the full force of her jealousy was directed at Helen because she's married to Theo. She called Helen to tell her Theo loves her. She admitted this and has no regrets.'

'So, who cut the car brakes of Helen's car?'

He gets up and starts pacing around the room. 'A few

days ago, you asked me to visit Helen in hospital. You said we should take it in turns, talk to her but I didn't know what to say. I was looking around for something to read to her and found a newspaper.'

I nod.

'It was a short article, with a photograph of a young man.' He pauses for a minute then looks at me. 'The person standing next to that young man is someone we both know.'

I quickly put my glass down and look at him. 'Who is it?'

'Don't be impatient.' He points to my glass. 'Look, you've spilt some.' He quickly drops a paper serviette over it, gives it a rub and chucks it in the bin, then goes to top up my glass.

'No thanks,' I say, covering my glass with my hand. 'So, who is the other person in the photo?'

'This is going to surprise you. The man in the photo is out on bail, suspected of drug trafficking.'

'And?'

'The person with him is James's wife.'

'Isabelle! But it's not long since James was murdered... why was she with this man?'

He gives a cynical laugh. 'I have a lawyer friend who knows about the case. This man is well-known by the police. Even worse, James's wife is staying with him in Piraeus. As you know, nobody recognized the person seen next to Helen's car. When we blew up the photo we had no success, but when I saw the photo in the newspaper, I knew I'd seen him somewhere before - same hat, same coat. So I looked at the photo of the man near Helen's car again - the lower half of his face is showing, then I knew it was him.'

I feel like going to Piraeus, I want to confront her. 'Who is this man, her boy-friend?'

'No, he's her brother. He stayed with James and Isabelle

when he first arrived from Columbia and that's when things started going wrong for James. Isabelle's brother was bringing people back to the house late at night. They were smoking joints and playing music loud. James asked him to stop, he wouldn't, so James told him he had to leave. This infuriated Isabelle and she took her brother's side. James didn't talk about it much, so I had no idea things were so bad.'

I feel a mixture of sadness and anger for James. 'Did Helen know about this?'

He shakes his head. 'I don't think so. He never said much to me and I can't see him telling Helen, she has enough problems of her own. The funny thing is Isabelle thought she'd inherit the lot when James died. Nice house in Faliron, the delicatessen, his share of Helen's business.'

'What a horrible woman!' I exclaim, 'How awful for James.'

'Yes, but James must have had his suspicions, he wasn't stupid, far from it.' He takes another sip of wine then in a confidential tone adds. 'He recently changed his will, all she gets now is the house.'

'Who gets the rest?' I have an idea but say nothing.

'I'm coming to that. The delicatessen goes to his sister and his share in Helen's travel business, plus any money from it, stays in Helen's business. Only if Helen dies and Isabelle doesn't remarry does it pass to her.'

'What if she re-marries?'

'It all goes to his sister.'

Now we're getting somewhere. 'Did she know about the change in his will?'

He shrugs. 'Who knows?'

'Maybe she found out and told her brother. Otherwise why would her brother cut Helen's brakes?'

'Isabelle swears she knew nothing about James changing his will, but we have our doubts.'

'What does her brother say?'

'His lawyer has instructed him to say nothing.'

There's a knock at the door, Dev stops and goes to open it.

In comes Helen followed by David.

As soon as she spots me she runs over. We sit chatting about Dev's news, then Helen asks us to come and see where they're staying in the hotel.

I can tell Dev doesn't really want to go, but what can we say, it's down to David that Dev's staying at the hotel. Of course it's stunning. From the balcony the view of Hyde Park during the day must be amazing. 'I wonder how much they charge for this,' I mumble to myself, 'it must be two grand a night, at least.'

David comes over and grins. 'Much more than I could ever afford, that's why it's good to have friends in the business. We're having dinner with some Spanish friends of mine tonight, would you both like to join us?'

'Can we do it another night?' asks Dev, 'I really need to talk to Beth, it's quite urgent.'

'Of course, but it'll have to be soon, I'm going back to Spain in a few days.'

'Come on David, time to go,' Helen says, giving me a knowing smile. 'We don't want to keep your friends waiting.' We say our goodbyes and they leave.

I'm waiting for Dev to finish what he was saying before Helen and David arrived, but he doesn't, what he does say surprises me.

'Shall we get something to eat?' he asks, picking up my coat from the bed. He holds it open for me and smiles. 'You must be hungry, I know I am.'

We jump in a taxi and drive to one of his favourite Italian restaurants in Charlotte Street.

It's not too busy when we arrive. Bottles of Chianti and paintings of Italy adorn the walls in the traditional Italian style. A waiter leads us to an alcove where there's a small round table with small table-lights that give it a feeling of romance which lightens our mood. I order mushroom risotto; Dev steak and sauté potatoes, we share a salad and a bottle of Chianti. For dessert I have a berry compote, Dev Italian ice-cream.

'Shall we go back to my hotel for coffee?' Dev asks, when we finish eating.

Of course, I say yes, I want him to finish what he was telling me earlier.

During dinner we just talked about things not related to the case and kept the atmosphere light.

Back at his hotel we're just about to order coffee in the bar when Dev's phone rings, it's Elias. By the look on his face I can tell something's wrong.

He frowns. 'Sorry, but I have to go.'

'Where, what's happened?'

'You know I can't tell you, I'll get a taxi and drop you off at home.'

We're soon speeding along Park Lane towards my apartment in a black London taxi. Dev waits till I'm safely inside, then the taxi drives off.

I slump down on the sofa, what the hell was Dev going to tell me. I sit thinking of what he said, then decide to call Elias. It's five to ten in London so nearly midnight in Athens. My call goes to voicemail, so I leave a message.

A few minutes later my phone rings, it's Elias.

'Beth, I got your message, is everything okay?'

'Yes, and no,' I mumble, not wanting to go into detail.

'Elias, I need to know what's happening, I was with Dev and it was going okay, then you called him. Where did he go? What's happening?'

'I can't tell you Beth, I am sworn to secrecy. I already said too much and Dev made me promise.'

As much as I try to get it out of him, he refuses to budge and says he'll call me tomorrow. I sit thinking about the past few hours and I know, something's very wrong, he's told me a lot, but he hasn't told me why he's here in London. Then I remember the letter, the letter I found with the name Fivos Demoulakis written on it which I'd circled in red. I forgot to tell Dev.

Grabbing my phone, I give him a call, it goes to voice-mail, so I send him a text.

Dev, I forgot to tell you something, it's probably just a coincidence but I think you should know. It's about the guy who was killed with James. This afternoon, I found an old letter from my ex and written on the envelope was a phone number, and next to it was the name Fivos Demoulakis. I now remember why I wrote it. Last year my ex called me and asked if I had the number of a friend of his. He said I also knew him and that they were in the same year at university in Athens. Anyway, there are lots of people with the same name, it's probably not important. Thanks for dinner. Take care. Beth

After reading it through I quickly delete the last two words and instead end with just Beth, then I press SEND.

It's still early and my mind's buzzing so I decide to phone my ex and see what he has to say about Fivos.

'Beth, I can't believe it's you,' he exclaims, sounding really surprised. 'How are you? And how is our son Jamie?'

'Jamie's fine, and so am I - I'm sorry to call so late, but I wanted to ask you something.'

I hear him laugh at the other end. 'I thought it was too good to be true, how can I help?'

I take a deep breath, I have to ask, don't I? 'Alex, the last time we spoke, you asked if I had the number of a friend of yours called Fivos.'

I must have surprised him as there's a big pause at the other end of the phone, I quickly add. 'You said he was a friend of ours and at the time I didn't remember who he was.'

'I don't know who you're talking about,' he replies, quickly, 'but I'm coming to London, tomorrow on business. I'll give you a call, we can meet at my hotel and talk about it then if you like?'

Now it's my turn to be surprised. We hardly ever speak, just when we have to. 'Okay, call me tomorrow when you get here, we'll arrange something.'

I sit thinking about Alex, then I think of Limonides. I wonder if Alex is still his lawyer? I shudder remembering things I want to forget. I'll meet Alex for a drink tomorrow, ask him about this guy Fivos and that will be the end of it.

32

BETH

LONDON

I JUST FINISHED DISCUSSING my article on Greece with my editor at their offices in High Holborn. She wants me to make changes I'm not happy about but what can I do? I didn't have time for breakfast so I'm walking in the direction of Covent Garden, I'll get a jacket potato, or some falafel, then go home.

On my way I check my phone for messages, I have two - one from Alex and another from Dev. Alex says he'll be at the Royal Garden Hotel in Kensington, around 7.30. He's only here for a day or two so wants to see Jamie. Mum won't be happy, not after what happened in Athens.

I read on with a sinking heart. He says he's going to call Jamie and may visit him in Oxford. Shit, that's done it, now what *am* I going to do?

I listen to Dev's message, he wants to see me, but much later - 8.30 at his hotel. If I get a move on, I should be able to see them both. Dev's phone is busy, so I send him a text confirming I'll be at his hotel tonight at 8.30.

After grabbing a pitta stuffed with falafel, I take the Tube home. The traffic in London is bad at most times, but at this time of the day it's even worse.

Back at home I shower then slip on a black pair of trousers, a dark gray evening style jumper, black boots and my warm black hooded coat. A spray of my favourite perfume, then I'm off.

It's 7.00 pm in the evening and pitch-black outside, it's also very cold. I try hailing a passing cab but it's full, they're all full, I should've booked one earlier, too late now. Shit I'm going to be late. Shall I phone for an Uber or walk up Queensway to the Bayswater Road.

I start walking and a vacant cab miraculously appears.

Everything's great until we reach Notting Hill then we hit traffic. Kensington Church Street is usually choc a bloc with traffic but tonight it's particularly bad.

'Driver, can you stop? I'll walk from here.'

It's late when I arrive at the hotel, my face is red from the cold, and I'm out of breath. I walk over to the bar, Alex is already there, he turns and sees me.

'Beth,' he calls, beckoning me over. 'You're late.'

He looks good – in fact just the same as usual. He pulls out the stool next to him. 'How was your trip to Athens?' he asks, in his usual laid-back way.

'Fine,' I reply, looking at him closely. It feels very strange being here with him. I haven't seen him since I left Athens.

I take off my coat and we sit for a while in silence. The last time we saw each other things were very bad, I'm sure he had something to do with that awful man Limonides, but I could never prove it.

He calls the barman over. 'What would you like to drink Beth, your usual?'

'Yes.'

'Sauvignon blanc and another whisky for me,' he says.

The barman nods.

Alex turns to me, a serious look on his face. 'How is Helen?'

I shrug. 'She's okay?' I can tell by his face he knows about her car crash, but I don't mention it. I wonder if he also knows about James. I'm just about to ask when he starts talking about our son Jamie and how much he's looking forward to seeing him. I'm trying hard to think of something to put him off when he changes the subject and starts talking about some of the cases he's working on.

'Sorry,' he suddenly exclaims, giving me an apologetic look. 'Here I am rambling on about work and you must be hungry. We can eat in the restaurant or in here if you like?'

'I'm not hungry,' I murmur, 'but don't let me stop you ordering.'

'No, it's too early for me. I just thought you might be hungry. By the way, I remember the guy you were talking about. I'd lost his phone number.'

The barman places my wine in front of me I take a couple of big gulps.

'Don't you remember him? He studied law with me. We met him a couple of times at the university re-unions.'

'That was a long time ago Alex.' I glance at my phone, it's nearly 8.30.

'Someone told me he'd been involved in a shooting in Athens,' Alex suddenly says, raising his hand to get the barman's attention.

I stare at him in astonishment, then glance at my phone. Shit. I'm going to be late.

I stand up to go. 'I'm sorry Alex, but I've got to be somewhere, I didn't realize how late it was.'

'Why so sudden?' he exclaims, then raises an eyebrow in mock surprise. 'The next time you're in Athens you must come to our apartment.'

I don't say anything, he carries on.

'And bring our son Jamie.'

I nod.

I leave him ordering a steak sandwich. It's late, shall I call Dev?

A taxi pulls up outside the hotel, I run to get it. 'Venus Hotel in Park Lane, quickly please.'

I feel someone hovering behind me so get inside before they grab it. The taxi driver smiles, switches his yellow light off and drives to Park Lane.

33

BETH & DEV

VENUS HOTEL, Park Lane
London

DEV'S IN THE BAR, he looks up and seems relieved to see me. 'How was your day?' he asks, pulling out a chair for me.

'Don't ask. I had to see my editor.'

'How's the job?'

I shrug. 'If I could find something better I'd leave.'

We sit talking about my job, but I'm desperate to know what happened last night, and he knows it.

'Dev, what happened last night?'

He shakes his head and frowns. 'Later Beth.'

He picks up a menu and looks at me. 'Are you hungry?'

'No.'

He smiles. 'Have something small to keep me company.' He hands me a menu and starts looking at his.

I glance quickly through the starters, they look good. 'Okay, I'll have the Mediterranean starter - cous-cous with feta, olives and peppers.'

'What to drink, red or white?'

'It's cold outside so a Pinot Noir would be nice.'

'So that's why you drink Sauvignon Blanc in Athens?'

I shrug. 'Yes, and no, it really depends on how I feel and tonight I feel like something with a bit of depth to it.'

He orders my starter, steak and chips for him and a bottle of Pinot Noir. It's strange how relaxed I feel. I wish he was always like this. It's a long time since I got on so well with someone, if only he would stay like this.

'Did you know that you're being followed?' he asks, sipping his wine.

I'm not really surprised. I had a strange feeling about the guy behind me at the hotel when I was getting into the taxi just now.

'Do you have them following me in London?'

He nods to the waiter to put the bill on his account.

'Let's finish this, then we can go to my room, we need to talk.'

At last, now I'll find out about last night.

He looks serious but says nothing as we take the elevator to his floor. As we walk along the corridor, he leans towards me and quietly says, 'You're being followed by us, but there are other people also following you.'

Opening the door to his room, he gestures for me to sit down. 'We know where you've been. This evening you went to the Royal Garden Hotel, then you were followed back here.'

I walk over to the French windows and gaze at the lights of London. 'So, who else is following me, do you know?'

'That's what we're trying to find out. Now you must be very careful, don't go anywhere alone.'

I turn and look at him. 'So, you're giving me a bodyguard?' I say, raising an eyebrow in mock surprise.

He shrugs. 'I told you not to get involved.'

I knew it wouldn't last, he's suddenly reverted to the old Dev.

'Did you get the text I sent you?' I ask.

'Yes, but you didn't say you were going to see your ex husband.'

'Why should I?'

He walks over to the small fridge and gestures for me to sit down. 'So, how is he?' he asks, studying the drinks in the fridge.

'He's okay,' I reply, opening the door to the balcony and breathing in the cold air.

'And?'

I shrug. 'We talked about Athens, he asked after Helen.'

He rubs his forehead, then locks eyes with me. 'You said you might know the person who was killed, with James?'

'Yes,' I step back into the room. 'The other night I called Alex to find out if he remembered asking me about one of his friends the last time he was in London.'

'What did he say?'

'At the time he said he didn't remember, but when I saw him tonight, he said he did. They were at university together and studied law, he was trying to contact him, that's why he called me. He said we used to see him at the student reunions.'

Dev's got his mask like face back, and he's watching me intently.

I turn to look out of the window to avoid his eyes.

'And?' he asks, impatiently.

'When I saw him tonight, he said he'd heard he was involved in a shooting incident, in Athens.' I wait for him to say something, but he says nothing, so I turn and look at him.

He's standing staring at me, his lips are clenched, his eyes an icy shade of blue. 'Beth, nobody knows the identity of the man except forensics, Elias and me.'

My mouth's dry, I swallow. He's right, how does Alex know?

'How did you know Fivos Demoulakis was his name?' he demands, in a harsh voice. 'You said you found something with Alex's phone number and the name Fivos written underneath in your handwriting.'

I nod, irritated by his manner.

'So how did you know this was the name of the man who was killed with James?'

'I told you,' I reply, angrily, knowing full well I'm in trouble. I don't want to involve Elias so garble the first thing that comes into my head. 'Alex called me last year and asked if I had this guy's number, I said I didn't but just in case I remembered I wrote Alex's number and the name of his friend on one of his old envelopes.' I roll my eyes and shrug. 'I said I'd call him if I found it - it's just a coincidence that it's the same name as...'

He raises an eyebrow, I can tell he's angry. 'All you've told me is that Fivos's name was on an old envelope, in your writing,' he snaps. 'But only forensics, Elias and I know the name of the man who was killed with James.'

Trying to appear as relaxed as possible, which I'm not, I sit down, cross my legs and take a sip of wine. 'Well if you must know, I asked Elias,' I reply, not looking at him. 'It was only because I kept pressing him to tell me. He said he shouldn't, but I insisted...'

'And why did you do that?' he asks, through clenched teeth. He comes over and peers into my face, forcing me to look at him.

I shrug and carry on drinking my wine, ignoring him.

He walks away, then turns around. 'Beth, I want to know how your ex knows Fivos was involved in the shooting, simple as that, do you know?'

I nearly choke on a mouthful of wine, but he just carries on talking.

'When we received the report from forensics and knew his identity, we checked Fivos Demoulakis out. Where he studied, where he worked, who his friends were etc., etc., and guess what? One of his friends was Alex, and Alex is very political, did you know that?'

He sits down opposite me and watches me intently.

I shrug and sip my wine. 'He was always political,' I reply, trying to appear casual. 'Most Greeks are.'

Dev stares at me. 'Over the past few years, Alex's political affiliation has changed, did you know?'

'How would I? I rarely speak to him, tonight was the first time I've seen him since I left Athens last year.'

He walks onto the balcony, takes out his phone and speaks quietly to Elias.

My phone rings. I stare at it, willing it to stop. It does but then it rings again, I ignore it. Dev comes running in, looks at my phone and sees Alex's name.

With his finger to his lips he gestures for me to answer.

'Hi Beth, I'm going to Oxford tomorrow. Would you like to come? We can see your mother and Jamie – what do you think?'

'No, I can't,' I mumble. 'Sorry, but I'm very busy.'

'Okay, maybe next time. I'll say hello for you.'

Great! That's all I need. I must let Jamie and Mum know. Putting down my phone, I turn and glare at Dev.

He shakes his head and shrugs. 'We only heard back from forensics yesterday, so you tell me. How does Alex know about Fivos?'

I sit staring at him. 'You don't really think Alex had something to do with James's murder, do you?'

He shrugs and for a moment looks very tired. 'We have to take him in for questioning, don't we?' He walks over to the balcony, speaks quietly in his phone then walks over to me. 'They've gone to pick him up at his hotel.'

I feel myself stiffen. I can't believe he just said that.

'We already picked up the guy who was following you,' he adds, watching me. 'I'll call Helen, you can stay with her tonight.'

I stand glaring at him. 'Why call Helen? I'm not staying here. I know Alex isn't a saint but he's not a murderer.'

He doesn't say anything, just picks up his phone and calls Helen.

Then he comes over to me, puts his hand on arm and quietly says. 'This is for the best, Beth.'

I shake his hand off of me. 'Just because Alex knows about it, doesn't mean he had anything to do with it, and...' I stop and take a deep breath. 'And I'm not staying here, I'm going home.'

He gives me a gentle shake. 'You must stay here. Surely you understand.'

I ignore him, my throat's dry, I look around for my wine.

'We have to take him in for questioning. We have to find out if he's involved, don't you want to know?'

I don't say anything.

He tries again. 'Beth, if he's innocent, he has nothing to worry about.' He picks up my coat. 'I'm taking you to

Helen's. There's a spare room where you can try to sleep, I'll call you in the morning.'

'No,' I hiss, glaring at him. 'I'm going home.'

'Why are you making this so damn difficult,' he snaps. 'I'm only thinking of you?'

Eventually he talks me into staying at the hotel, he says he won't have to worry about me being alone in my apartment, and as he's staying at the hotel, it makes sense if I'm here also.

Helen opens the door to their suite, we go inside then Dev's phone rings, it's Elias. He turns and talks quietly to him, then he looks at me.

'I'm going, okay?'

'Call me, I want to know if...'

He nods and walks back to the elevator, still talking to Elias.

34

BETH

VENUS HOTEL, Park Lane
London

AS SOON AS I open my eyes, the previous night's events come flooding back to me, I'm at the Venus hotel in Park Lane.

My feet sink into the thick pile of the hotel carpet as I slide out of bed. It's so quiet, is everyone asleep?

I slowly pad into the kitchen and see Helen drinking coffee. She looks up and pulls out a chair.

'Come and sit down, now it's my turn to look after you.' She pats the seat next to her. 'I'll make us some breakfast.'

After pouring me a coffee and making some toast, we sit sipping coffee. She bites into a thick slice of buttered toast, butter oozes down her mouth, she wipes it off with a serviette.

'We've got to stay together, Beth, see this through, I'm going back to Athens soon, want to come with me?'

I look at her and frown. 'What about Jamie, he's staying with Mum for a few days, but if I come back to Athens with you, I'll have to ask Mum if she can stay with Jamie, he has to go back to school, and...'

'Beth don't worry, I'll come with you to Oxford, you go and see your Mum and Jamie, I'll check on the house in Evesly. I'm still not sure if I want to sell it or keep it. Anyway, I have to be back in Athens in two days for the divorce hearing.'

Helen pushes the plate of toast towards me. 'Eat something, then we'll get ready.'

'Okay, what time's the next train from Paddington?'

She scans the timetable on her phone. 'It's 11.10 we can make it if we hurry.'

She's already dressed and starts making a list of things to check in her house. She hasn't visited the house since...

It was last September, I'd just left Alex, I came to stay with Mum in Oxford.

'I wonder if any work needs doing,' she murmurs, staring into space. 'I'll call the agent she can meet me outside the house.' She stops suddenly...

'Sorry Beth, I wasn't thinking...'

'Don't worry Helen, I've forgotten all about it.' I haven't really, I still have nightmares thinking about those men and what happened later. Helen's house is in Evesly, a small village just a twenty-minute train ride from the centre of Oxford, it's a place I never want to return to. I look over at Helen, she looks so worried.

'I'll give Mum a call, let her know we're coming.'

'Great, I'll get a taxi to take us to the station.'

Five minutes later the hotel phone rings.

'Taxi's downstairs, come on.'

With just ten minutes to spare, we arrive at the station, grab our tickets from the machine, get on the train and settle down for the one-hour journey to Oxford.

The familiar stops along the way bring back memories of James, I still can't believe he's gone.

'We have to find out who killed him,' Helen says quietly, brushing a tear from her face.

I nod. 'Don't worry, we will.'

Mum's house is a fifteen-minute walk from the station,

Helen decides to get out with me. 'I'm not hanging around here for the next train to Evesly,' she remarks, walking to the exit with me.

I can't help but laugh. 'I didn't think you would.' Helen hates changing trains.

'I'll take a taxi to Evesly,' she says, giving me a wink. 'Much easier and quicker.'

'Are you sure you'll be alright?'

'Of course, say hello to your Mum and Jamie for me. I'll let you know when I'm leaving.'

'Okay.' As I walk to Mum's I start thinking about Jamie. He's slight for his age, with dark air like his father and green eyes like me. Memories of last night and what Dev said about Alex won't go away.

'Beth!'

I look up and see Mum taking some shopping bags from her car.

'Hey Mum,' I call, running over and giving her a hug.

'Here let me help you.'

'It's good to see you Beth, how was Athens?'

'I'll tell you all about it in a minute.'

Mum doesn't know about James, but I don't want to talk about it in front of Jamie.

She looks anxiously at me. 'Are you sure you're alright?'

I laugh. 'Of course.' She never changes she can read me like a book. It seems ages since I left Athens and came to Oxford. My divorce was just going through, Jamie was only eleven, well going on twelve. The last few months seem to have gone very quickly.

She grabs a bag from me and pulls me along the path. 'Come on let's have coffee.'

It's quiet inside. 'Where's Jamie?'

'Oh, he's gone to the corner shop to buy some bread, we forgot to get some at the supermarket.'

While Jamie's out I quickly update Mum with the recent events in Athens. Some of the things I leave out, but not many. Mum says she hasn't heard from Alex and she's sure he hasn't called Jamie.

Just then the front door opens and in comes Jamie with the bread.

'Mum!'

He comes over and hugs me. 'I've missed you, how's Athens?'

'The same as usual, the weather's much better than here, it's more like spring than winter.'

I know Jamie often thinks about Athens, he's made a few friends at the school he goes too in London, but he still misses his friends in Greece.

'Shall we go to the café for some coffee and cakes?' I ask. 'I don't have long, I'm going back to Athens with Helen soon.'

Jamie's face falls. 'Is everything alright Mum?'

I laugh. 'Everything's alright, I'm just going to help Helen with her divorce. And don't worry, Nan's coming back to London with you, she's staying with us for a while.' I'm wondering if he's heard from his dad, but he's said nothing.

Dev said they were going to pick Alex up from his hotel, so where have they taken him?

My phone rings, it's Helen, she says she'll be at Oxford station in about an hour.

'Helen's meeting me outside the station in an hour so shall we go Café Loco?'

We bundle into Mum's car and drive to the café. Jamie chooses a large chocolate eclair, Mum and I have a toasted teacake and a large pot of tea - Jamie has a bottle or sparkling orange. We sit chatting about the view of Christchurch Cathedral from one of the windows.

'Do you remember that Harry Potter tour I wanted to go on Mum? Some of the filming was done here.'

'Yes, of course I remember.'

It was the day after Mum's house was firebombed, how could I forget, we spent most of the day shopping.

My phone rings, it's Helen, she'll be at the station in ten minutes.

'Sorry but I have to go, Helen's nearly at the station.'

As Mum drives us to the station she gives me a sideways look. 'Don't worry Beth, I'll get our stuff packed tonight, we'll be back in London tomorrow.'

After lots of hugs and kisses I run into the station to meet Helen.

When we arrive back at the hotel David's in the kitchen cooking one of his favourite Spanish dishes.

'It's ready!' he beams, piling our plates with saffron spiced vegetable paella. 'Can you get the wine, red's on the top of the fridge, white's inside.'

'Who taught you to cook like this?' I ask, swallowing the last mouthful of paella.

'Nobody really, I spent a lot of time helping out in the restaurant when I was young. I just sort of picked it up, I enjoy cooking.'

I look over at Helen, she hates cooking.

She gives me one of her exasperated looks and clears away the plates, I make coffee.

David's on his phone to his sister in Spain, then mine rings, it's Dev.

'Did you notice if you were followed today?' he asks, quickly.

'I don't think so,' I reply, surprised by the urgency in his voice.

'We have to be sure. I want you to stay with Helen and David, until this is over.'

'I can't, I have a meeting with my editor tomorrow.'

'See your editor tomorrow but then nothing more. Take Helen or David with you and get them to wait outside, this is serious, Beth, these people are dangerous.'

He hangs up leaving me speechless. I wanted to ask him if Alex has been arrested, he knew I wanted to ask him, that's why he put the phone down.

Just then Helen comes over and whispers in my ear. 'Don't worry! I'll come with you tomorrow. I'll wait for you in that lovely café near your editor's building.'

I swing round. 'Did Dev call you?'

She nods. 'As I said this morning Beth, it's my turn to look after you now.'

35

DEV

HQ - Athens - Midnight

Dev notices the lights are on in Katia's office.

'What are you doing here,' he asks, opening the door. 'It's late?'

'We have so much work to do,' she mumbles, clicking on her screen. 'I've been very busy, Dev.'

He walks over to her chair and peers at the screen. 'Any updates on Alex Papadakis?'

'Yes, the political party he belongs to has been under surveillance for months.'

She turns and looks at him. 'But you know that already, don't you?'

He nods. 'Well let me know if you find anything else, it's very urgent.'

Dev yawns, looks at his phone, it's just gone midnight. 'I've had a long day I think I'll call it a day.'

Katia walks over and drapes an arm around his shoulder. 'I've some information you might find interesting.'

She leans closer to him. He can feel her warm body against his and gently pushes her away. She shrugs, playfully squeezes his thigh then moves her hand higher to his crotch.

'Katia!'

'But I know you like it,' she murmurs, fondling him, I can tell. Then she grabs his hand and pushes it between her legs, she has no panties on.

'Not here,' he snaps. He walks over to the water dispenser, takes a plastic cup and fills it with water.

'Okay, okay,' she laughs. 'I can wait.'

With a deep sigh, Dev drinks the water. He enjoys having sex with Katia, but not now that she's back with her husband.

Crushing the polystyrene cup in half, he turns and flings it into the bin.

Katia goes back to her computer. 'Okay, now this is serious,' she says, peering at him over the top of her glasses. 'This can be very good for us, it can work to our advantage, but we must play our cards right.'

He nods. Katia has an excellent mind, she's a brilliant mathematician, but she can also be very devious and crafty which often works to their advantage.

'I've been checking their organization or party, whatever you want to call it,' she says, in a matter of fact voice. 'It goes by the name of DEMOS.' She pauses, raises an eyebrow, then looks at Dev. 'Now here's the interesting bit. One of their members was recently kicked out of the party.'

'Do you know his name?' Dev asks, looking at her screen.

'His name is Mario, he's very young, about nineteen, he's a bit of a live wire.' She turns and smiles at Dev. 'You know the type, he doesn't take well to rules and regulations and that sort of thing. Anyway, he wouldn't follow the party line, so they booted him out.'

Dev's mind is working fast. This could be what they've been waiting for. 'Excellent,' he mutters. 'We've been trying to get one of our undercover agents to infiltrate them for some time now.'

After a few seconds he looks at her. 'Get one of our agents to befriend this Mario.'

She nods, all ears now.

'We need to find out about the members of the club,' he mutters as if to himself. 'We need someone who can behave as if they sympathize with his situation.'

'Who shall we send,' she asks, peering into his face.

He walks over to a computer, taps in a few words and a list of agent's names appear. Scanning through them quickly he clicks into a couple of the profiles, then turns to Katia.

'I think Demetri will be good. He's young, easy to get along with and he has a good track record.'

Katia looks happy. 'Good, shall I contact him now?'

'Yes, find out if he's up to it, make sure he's a hundred percent sure he knows how to handle the situation. Tell him to take his time, give him all the background information he needs especially Mario's political views, and tell him to be very careful.'

Katia nods.

'I'm going home now to grab some sleep.'

Katia looks at him with a knowing smile and gestures for him to call her.

Dev smiles, her husband must be away tonight on business or whatever it is he gets up too. He opens the door to leave. 'Okay, call me if it's urgent.'

An hour later he's in the shower feeling more relaxed. His phone rings, it's on the basin outside the shower, he pokes out his head - it's Katia's number.

'Good news!' she says as soon as he answers. 'Demetri has made contact - they're having drinks at a bar off Omonia Square. Maybe we won't have to wait long.'

He smiles to himself. She's a fast worker in more ways than one. There's a slight tap on his front door, he stops and listens, he's not expecting anyone.

Wrapping a towel around his waist he makes his way to the door. There it goes again, this time it's much louder. Wondering who it can be at just gone 1.00 am in the morning, he tightens the towel around his waist and looks through the spy hole.

Katia's outside on her phone, he frowns and opens it. 'What's wrong?'

She walks inside, takes off her long black coat and throws it over a chair.

Dev shakes his head and smiles - she's totally naked.

She loosens her hair, kicks off her boots and slowly walks into his bedroom.

With a deep sigh, he follows her.

36

DEV'S APARTMENT

10.16 am

It's late when he wakes up. He shoots out of bed furious with himself for oversleeping, he should have known what she was up to last night. She's a beautiful woman, but also a married woman, this cannot be repeated.

He heads for the shower, turns it on full blast to ease his aching body.

Katia's already showered, dressed and having coffee.

Ten minutes later Dev comes into the kitchen, gulps down a few sips of black coffee and they leave.

Katia takes a cab to HQ, Dev slides into his car. On the way he calls Demetri to find out what happened last night. The news is good.

'We got on well,' Demetri replies, excitedly. 'We had a couple of drinks and Mario slowly opened up, he's feeling pissed off and after a few more drinks... well I was able to get all the information we need.'

'Excellent! Did he say anything about the members?'

'Yes, he thinks they're a bunch of weirdos.' He hesitates to take another drag of his cigarette, then mutters. 'Then he told me something really interesting.'

'What?'

'It seems Alex was already suspicious of Fivos, he invited him for a drink, then planted a bug on him.'

'How does he know this?'

'He was there, he saw Alex lean across Fivos, he thought he was reaching for an ash tray, but then he saw him plant the bug on Fivos's jacket.'

Dev draws in a deep breath. This is beyond his wildest expectations. 'What else did he say?'

Demetri takes another drag, then carries on. 'He said Alex knew Fivos was talking to the members, many people complained about him, they said he was a mole, that's why he put the bug on him. Fivos wasn't a member and Alex wanted to know what he was up to.' He stops and stubs out his cigarette. 'He caught him eavesdropping himself and was furious.'

'What else?'

'Only a few of them knew about this, including Mario. Alex swore them all to secrecy, he instructed them to say nothing to anyone. For a couple of days, they listened in to Fivos's conversations via the bug, but then the conversations stopped so they presumed he'd found it.'

'Did you tape what he said?' Dev had specifically told Katia to make sure he did this. He drives slowly along Syntagma waiting for Demetri's reply.

Demetri laughs. 'Of course, Katia told me to do this. There were CCTV cameras near the bar and in the room, so we've got him on camera and on tape.'

'Excellent, bring him in, show him the footage and let

him listen to the tape. And tell him we'll go easy on him if he tells us everything.'

Dev stops off at a small café for a slice of toast and two strong black coffees. He makes a couple of phone calls then leaves.

As he arrives back at HQ, he spots Katia leaving with Jonathan the lawyer. He watches as she slides into Jonathan's car.

She sees him and waves. 'We're going to the police station.'

He sticks his head out of his window. 'I need to check the statements made by Alex Papadakis.'

Jonathan's car speeds off with a screech of tires, Dev follows them.

When they arrive Jonathan and Katia go to see the Head of Police, Dev goes to check Alex's statement. His eyebrows shoot up as he reads it. Alex says someone told him Fivos had been killed, but he couldn't remember who.

His phone rings, it's Katia. 'I thought you might like to know they're questioning Mario.'

'Why didn't you tell me this earlier?' Dev demands, sharply.

'I didn't know,' Katia replies, just as frostily. 'I suggest you get over there now, I'm stuck here with Jonathan...'

Dev cuts her off and makes a beeline for the interrogation room. Fortunately, he hasn't missed much. He eases himself quietly into a chair at the side of the room and hits record on his phone.

It doesn't take long for Mario to realize he's in trouble. The detective says they'll go easy on him if he makes a signed statement telling them everything. At first, he refuses, they continue with the interrogation, he eventually agrees.

Taking out his phone Dev leaves the room to call Katia, no reply.

He calls the hospital where James and Fivos were taken on that fateful night. Fivos's body is still in the morgue.

'This is very important I want you to check his jacket, I think there may be a bug on it.'

Ten minutes later forensics call back, they found nothing on the jacket.

He starts pacing up and down the corridor then stops. Alex was voluntarily flown back to Athens to be questioned. So far, he's refused to say anything about the party members. He tries Katia again, this time she picks up.

'Any news about Alex?' he asks, this time not so sharply. 'Has he said anything?'

'You're just in time, he just gave us the names of the other members.'

'Excellent, thanks Katia.'

'Not at all boss,' she replies, then quickly adds. 'Anything, for you.'

He sits frowning thinking about Katia, he knows it can't go on but how to stop her? He shrugs and sits reading through his notes, he's missing something important but what? The CCTV footage outside the metro at Monesteraki was checked around the time Beth received the call. She'd seen the footage they had but didn't recognize anyone.

He takes out his phone. 'Katia, can you check if anymore CCTV footage has been found near the metro at Monesteraki?'

'Of course, I'll pop round later and update you with what we've found, then we can resume where we left off this morning.'

37

BETH & HELEN

VENUS HOTEL, Park Lane
London

I'M HAVING coffee with Helen when Mum calls, she says they'll be in London by about 3.30. As soon as I put my phone down it rings, it's Dev.

'Hi Beth, we've found some more CCTV footage from near the metro station in Monesteraki, around the time you received the phone call.'

'But I don't see how I can help?' I reply, surprised he should mention it. 'I don't even know what he looks like.'

'Yes, I know,' he snaps, irritably. 'I'll email some shots over for you to look at, but you'll have to come to Athens to view the CCTV footage.'

I glance over at Helen, I know she can hear what he's saying. I didn't know he was back in Athens, Helen and I had just been discussing getting flights. I called work and they're OK about me going. My editor wants me to get more information about the economic situation in Athens, which suits me fine.

'I thought it was too dangerous for me to be in Athens?' I say. 'What happened?'

He pauses for a while. 'I thought it would help, but if you can't, don't worry.'

I get the feeling he's holding something back. He hasn't told me what's happened about Alex.

'Listen, you haven't...'

'As I said, it can wait. Okay...'

'What can wait?' I snap.

'Well, if you really want to know, it's about Alex and his political party, or rather...'

'What party? What are you talking about?'

'Beth, I shouldn't be telling you this,' he mutters. 'It's highly confidential, if you know what I mean.'

'What is it?' He doesn't reply.

'Look Dev, you know you can trust me, I won't say anything.'

'Okay, but this is just between you and me, right?'

'Of course.'

'Your ex runs or helps run a political party, one of our agents befriended a young guy Alex kicked out and we've gained some valuable information.'

'What information?'

'It's about Fivos, the man your ex contacted you about, remember, the man who was murdered with James?'

Helen's sitting next to me, she can hear everything, she doesn't know about Fivos. I don't reply. He carries on talking.

'It seems Alex was suspicious of Fivos, he suspected him

of being a mole so had him bugged. It worked for a couple of days then it stopped, he must have found the bug, or it fell off. I checked with the morgue but there's no bug on his jacket.'

'So, where is Alex?'

'He's here in Athens. The police are questioning him, they asked him for the names of the other members who knew about this.'

'Did he tell them?'

'It took a while but eventually he did.'

I sit for a while trying to digest this, I know Alex has changed, but he would never kill anyone, would he?

'So, are they charging Alex with anything?'

He doesn't reply. Helen sits staring at me visibly shaken.

'Okay. I'll book a flight. I'll call you when I'm in Athens.'

'Let me know which flight you're on, I'll try and collect you from the airport.'

I close my phone, go out onto the balcony and take a deep breath.

'Are you okay?' Helen asks, coming out onto the balcony to join me.

'Yes, just getting some air...'

She wraps an arm around my shoulder, we stand like this for a few minutes, saying nothing just looking at the traffic below, then she gives me a hug. 'I'm going inside to book some tickets for Athens - yes?'

I nod.

She grabs her phone.

A few minutes later we have two flights booked for the following morning, leaving at 8.15am.

I get up and start getting ready to leave. 'I have to go home, collect my things and get the place ready for Mum and Jamie.'

'Yes, and I must let David know we're leaving. He had an early morning appointment and isn't due back till later. I'll give him a call him now.'

I sit listening to her chat to David then start thinking about Alex. He has changed a lot, that's why I asked for a divorce, all those shady deals with Limonides, all that money he made which I didn't know about, and that woman...

I get up and walk to the window. That was the worst part of it all, I always had a feeling something was wrong.

Suddenly Helen looks over at me, she raises an eyebrow as if to ask if I'm okay, I nod and smile, she continues talking.

'That's great David.'

Then she puts the phone on speaker so I can hear what they're saying.

'When everything's over we'll visit you in Spain.'

'Great,' says David, I'll make sure you have the best rooms, and you won't have to pay, it's on the house, you'll both be very welcome.'

Helen looks happy.

'We'll definitely hold you to that, David.'

She closes her phone and looks at me. 'Make sure you keep Easter free as we're going to the Costa del Sol to see David.'

I laugh and put on my coat. 'I'm going to get my place ready before Mum and Jamie get there.'

She grabs her coat. 'I'm coming to I don't want to stay here by herself, I'll keep you company.'

Two minutes later, we're outside the hotel hailing down a taxi.

My apartment feels warm and cozy, it's just as I left it,

clothes are strewn all over the bed - I must tidy up before they get here.

'You pack, I'll make coffee,' Helen calls going into the kitchen.

'Yes, and this time I'm taking a large suitcase, no more carry-on luggage, just a large shoulder bag with my laptop, passport, purse and make-up inside it.'

When I've finished packing we sit drinking coffee, then I do a final check just to make sure I have everything I'll need, then we tidy up and get things ready for Mum and Jamie.

Ten minutes later they arrive. We sit chatting for a while, I don't tell them about Dev, they think I'm going to Athens to give Helen support with her divorce. After making sure Jamie has all he needs for school tomorrow, we go outside and get a taxi. Ten minutes later we're outside the hotel.

'We must check in two hours before take-off, Helen.'

She nods and pays the driver. 'I've arranged for an early morning call at 5.30 am.'

We run into the warm hotel and take the elevator to their suite.

While Helen has a quick shower, I take a small brandy from the fridge glug it down, then roll into bed.

38

BETH & HELEN

Next Morning - Venus Hotel, Park Lane
London

The early morning dawn clings to the air as we leave for the airport. David's fast asleep so we leave him a note and quietly tiptoe out of the suite.

As we leave the elevator the heavenly scent of breakfast wafts over to us from the breakfast room. I stop for a second. 'Mmmm, coffee...'

'Come on Beth,' Helen mutters. 'We have a plane to catch.'

Thirty minutes later we're checking in our luggage at Heathrow airport and going through customs. By now we're both in need of a strong coffee and something to eat. Pret A Manger seems to be the nearest café. It's already busy, so Helen grabs a table and I get breakfast.

After coffee and croissants we sit checking our emails, then it's time to board. With a few healthy snack bars stashed away in our bags, we settle down for the four-hour flight. The last call to switch off phones and laptops reminds me that I forgot to call Dev, I'll call him when we land.

Soon the plane is high in the sky, we're on our way back to Athens. We sleep for most of the journey. When we arrive I text Dev to let him know we're here - no reply, he must be busy.

We take the metro to Syntagma Square and from there we walk to the Plaka Hotel. With the two-hour difference it's late afternoon by the time we get there, Helen's exhausted and goes to her room to rest.

I'm on the balcony with an ice-cold beer checking my emails. There's one from Dev, he says he'll pop round to the hotel around 8.00ish tonight. Another email from Mum and Jamie asking me to call them when I arrive, which I do.

JUST LIKE OLD times we're sitting on the hotel terrace when Dev arrives, he looks tired and orders an espresso coffee.

'So, shall we start?' he asks, looking at me when he says this.

I take a sip of beer and nod.

'Well, as you probably know Alex has the best legal team in Greece working for him so he should be out on bail shortly.' He sits looking at us for a minute then carries on. 'The man who followed you in London has been picked up.'

I'm just about to ask for his name, when Dev adds. 'His name is Stavros Stamatis. He's being questioned now. Tomorrow you can check the latest CCTV footage, I'll collect you around 9 am tomorrow morning.'

He looks tired so I give him a reassuring smile. 'Yes, that's fine.'

He stands up to go. 'I was hoping we could all have dinner tonight, but unfortunately I have an appointment.' Then to my surprise he leans over and hugs me. 'See you tomorrow.' Then he's gone.

Of course, Helen hasn't missed it and gives me an impish smile but says nothing. She looks at the hotel menu then at me. 'What about Greek ravioli, chips and salad?'

'Sounds great.'

Soon we're tucking into bowls of ravioli and drinking a bottle of ice-cold white wine. I put down my now nearly empty glass of wine and look at Helen. 'You know, there's something everyone seems to be missing and I think it's very important.'

She looks surprised. 'What's that?'

'Dev said Alex had bugged Fivos, so he probably knows why James was going to see Fivos.'

She nods for me to carry on.

'We must listen to everything Alex recorded.'

'And how do you intend doing that?'

'I'm not sure, but there must be a way.'

She sits sipping her wine, then looks at me thoughtfully. 'Can Dev get access to them?'

I shrug.

She frowns. 'Maybe Alex has destroyed them, have you asked Dev?'

'No, but I'm going to.'

39

DEV & BETH

ATHENS - 9.11 AM in the morning

DEV PUSHES the old door just in the right place in the now familiar small street near the Acropolis, the door opens and in we go.

The buzz of computers fills the air as we enter their headquarters. On our way to the digital department we pass Katia. I feel her eyes boring into my back then she gets up and follows us into the room. She stands close to Dev with an arm around his shoulders in a protective sort of way. I'm surprised by this show of affection but pretend not to notice.

He gently shrugs off her arm and walks over to a table. 'This is very important, so listen.' He turns and gives me a reassuring smile. 'It's crucial you take your time and look carefully at the photos then at all the footage, Beth.' He pulls out a chair for me, so I sit down.

'I'll talk to you later,' he says, looking at Katia.

Her face clouds over, she shrugs and leaves us to get on with it.

Dev stands flicking through his phone, I start going through the photos then look at the CCTV footage.

After a while I go back to the photos and stop at one, he looks familiar. The mouth is thin, his features are fine. I'm sure I've seen him somewhere before, but where?

'Found anything?' Dev murmurs.

I hesitate for a minute, then point to the photo. 'This one looks familiar, but I'm not sure.' The more I look at it the less sure I become. Dev hasn't taken his eyes off me, I know how important this is to him. 'No, I'm really not sure, let's leave it.'

'Don't worry.' He peers over my shoulder at the photo and shrugs. 'You can always come back and see them again. I'll drive you back to your hotel.'

'It's nice of you to offer Dev,' I say as quietly as I can, 'but I want to walk.'

'Are you sure?'

'Yes.'

We leave the room.

On our way out we pass Katia, she pretends not to see us, but I know she's watching me, he walks with me to the elevator.

'I'll call you later, Beth.'

'Yes, let me know as soon as you have some news.'

He nods.

Soon I'm outside in the street just below the Acropolis. As I walk along, I think of Katia. She obviously has feelings for Dev, or maybe it's just my overactive imagination, but usually I'm right.

The sun sparkles through the leaves and throws rays of

light over the nearby cafés - I get a whiff of coffee and pastries - I'm hungry - I didn't have breakfast this morning. I hurry back to the hotel to see if Helen's up.

Dev sits flicking through the photos then stops and stares at one of them.

The door opens silently, Katia walks over to him.

'Who the hell was that?' she asks, leaning over so her face is close to his.

He jumps, swivels around in his chair and stares at her. 'Katia, you know we have to find this man and Beth is helping us.'

With her hands on her hips she looks at him angrily. 'I can see she was helping you.' Then leaning close to him she murmurs. 'Now it's my turn to help you.'

He can feel her warm sensuous body through her thin short dress and gently pushes her away.

His phone rings, it's the police, Alex is about to be interviewed and they want him there.

Grabbing his jacket, he leaves HQ and drives to the police station in Syntagma Square.

Standing behind the two-way glass Dev watches Alex enter the room, the interview begins.

'Did you plant the bug on Fivos's jacket?'

'Yes, I did,' replies Alex.

'Why?'

'I caught him eavesdropping. He was listening to conversations which didn't concern him. Naturally I wanted to know what he was up to and who he was working for.'

Dev notices how confident Alex is, he's not at all intimidated by being questioned, but there again, he's used to it, he's one of the leading criminal lawyers in Athens, this is nothing new to him.

'You heard him arrange to meet James at the bar by the beach,' the detective says. 'Are you denying you know about this?'

Alex frowns. 'No, I'm not denying it, but we also heard a lot of other things he said. We listened to his conversations for a few days and then they stopped. He must have found the bug and removed it.'

'So, you deny arranging for him to be killed?'

'Yes, of course.'

Dev's heard enough, he leaves the room and the police station, slides into his car and drives back to HQ. He starts thinking about the case, what is he missing? He starts going through it again. This morning Beth checked the new CCTV footage for the Monesteraki metro station area where the man called her from and saw nothing. There has to be something he's missing, but what?

40

HELEN'S DIVORCE

ATHENS - 10.30am

THE DAY of the divorce hearing finally arrives. Helen's wearing a dark gray suit, white blouse and black shoes. A dark pink silk scarf adds the finishing touch to her outfit.

I'm wearing a light gray suit with a pale blue blouse and my black boots as usual. For a change my flyaway blonde hair is brushed and held back with a clip.

With a feeling of trepidation, we enter the courtroom and the hearing begins. Theo isn't here.

Eventually the judge deems there are grounds for divorce, the photos and videos confirm beyond doubt that Theo has been unfaithful and guilty of mental cruelty. He orders Theo vacate the Kolonaki house immediately.

Helen's ecstatic with joy, I want to stand up and cheer, but of course I don't.

'Let's go to the rooftop bar at the Grande Bretagne Hotel,' she says, beaming with delight. 'This calls for a celebration, we can ask Dev and Elias to join us there for lunch.

An hour later we're all in the bar having lunch when Elias receives an urgent call to cover a breaking story.

'I'm so sorry I have to leave,' he says, giving us a worried look. 'I wish I could stay but...'

Helen laughs. 'Don't worry Elias, we'll do this again, now hurry or you'll be late.'

After coffee Dev walks us back to the hotel.

As soon as we arrive Helen heads for the elevator. 'I need to have a rest, but don't let me stop you two from having a drink on the terrace.'

Dev looks at me. 'That's a good idea, shall we?'

I'm sure there's a glint of amusement in his eyes, they look very blue today. Helen gives me an impish grin and disappears into the elevator.

'Would you like to go somewhere else for a change?' he asks. 'There's a bar I know, it's only a ten-minute walk from here.'

Now this is the Dev I like. 'Okay, lead the way.' Let's hope he doesn't get any phone calls to distract him like the last time.

The bar is small, low lights, with soft Greek music playing in the background. There's a corner seat which offers more privacy than the others which we grab.

A waiter comes over to takes our order. Two minutes later he returns with a bottle of red and two glasses which he fills to the top.

Dev clinks glasses with me and smiles. 'So, when are you going back to London?'

I look at him over the rim of my glass. 'I'm not sure.'

'What about Helen? Is she going back to sort out her house?'

'Yes, but we won't be going back until James's case is solved.'

He looks surprised. 'But it could be a long time before...'

'Dev, I want to ask you something, can you get me the tapes of the bugged conversations Alex made of Fivos?'

He chokes on his drink, hastily gropes for a serviette and wipes his mouth.

'You are joking of course!'

'Of course I'm not joking,' I snap. 'I thought you wanted to solve this case.' He raises an eyebrow and shakes his head, I've seen him do this a lot recently, so just ignore him.

I lean forward and look at him. 'You're missing something very important and I think you know what I'm talking about.'

He sits watching me but says nothing, there's the hint of a smile on his lips.

'The guy who phoned me from outside the metro at Monesteraki, you haven't found, him have you?' I can see I've hit a sore spot and smile. 'He's the missing link, isn't he?'

He sits drinking his wine, but I can tell he wants to hear more.

'You hauled me off to Mont Parnes to identify someone and ended up getting poisoned - they're out to get all of us, aren't they?'

He's watching me intently but says nothing, I carry on. 'It's the warning I received from the guy who called me at the hotel, don't you remember? He told me to stop putting my nose into things that don't concern me.'

He raises an eyebrow but still says nothing.

As an afterthought I add. 'Oh, and by the way, I forgot to tell you, someone attacked me when I left you and Elias at the restaurant that night, he had a very long knife, I was lucky someone came along and scared him off.'

I can see him stiffen, he's furious I haven't said anything about this before. If it wasn't so serious, I'd burst out laughing, but I don't, I take a sip of wine and wait.

He sits watching me with that mask like face, his eyes like slits of blue. 'You're right, Beth, but you've seen all the photos and the new CCTV footage and you noticed nothing.'

I nod and put my glass down, he leans forward, takes the bottle of wine and tops up our glasses.

'I was thinking about this the other night Dev and there is an easy way to find out who the killer is.'

He rolls his eyes up to the ceiling and laughs. 'Now this is something I want to hear.'

I smile because I know he's going to like what I say. 'Okay. Alex gave the police the names of the other members who heard these tapes and you have their names, yes?'

He nods.

'Can you get the recordings of these party meetings?'

He shrugs.

'This is very important, get the recordings and videos of their meetings...' I lower my voice and move closer to him, our faces are practically touching. 'And I might be able to recognize the voice of the man on the phone, then...' I take a sip of wine, he sits waiting. 'If I can see a few videos of their meetings...well, it makes it so much easier for me, doesn't it?'

I sit back enjoying the expression on his face. 'Ask Alex, for the videos and recordings, tell him that if we find out who killed James, he'll be in the clear.'

He sits silently watching me then takes out his phone. He asks to speak to Alex. The police tell him he's out on bail, so he calls his mobile.

'Alex, this is Dev. If you want to clear yourself, I think I can help.'

I can hear Alex laugh at the other end, Dev carries on talking.

'Get me the recordings and videos of your party meetings where the men you named are present. This is urgent.'

Alex doesn't sound very happy about it, I can hear him making excuses.

'I don't care if it is short notice,' Dev hisses. 'Send them to Takis's bar by special delivery, it's just off Syntagma Square, or bring them yourself.'

Shit, I didn't expect him to invite him here. We sit sipping our wine, waiting.

Ten minutes later Alex calls Dev to say he's sending them over by special delivery to the bar.

Fifteen minutes pass and still no delivery. Dev doesn't say much just sits flicking through his phone.

Suddenly a man walks into the bar, he stands looking around then comes over to us. He's obviously been given Dev's description. He's holding a small parcel.

Dev shows him some ID, then the man hands him the small package and leaves.

'Come on,' Dev mutters, standing up, 'My car's outside.'

We leave the bar and drive along the busy streets of Athens towards the Acropolis.

Once again we go through the old door and down the elevator into the bowels of this amazing building. As soon as we're in the digital room Dev opens the small package, inside are video recordings and tapes.

We sit watching the videos which at first are interesting then get a bit boring. Dev starts pacing up and down the room, I close my eyes and listen.

Then it happens.

'That's the voice, play it back!'

Dev runs over, rewinds the video just a little then presses play.

'Yes that's him.'

I open my eyes and look at the screen, the man is tall, with longish dark hair, I've never seen him before. I sit staring at him. 'Rewind it. I want to make sure.'

We watch the video several more times, then Dev takes a snapshot of the man. He searches through their database and eventually finds him, his name is Demos Gramaticos, he lives in Piraeus.

'Come on, Beth, I'll drive you back to your hotel.'

I look at him in surprise. 'Can't I come to Piraeus with you?'

He shrugs. 'Sorry, but we must do this without you.'

Within minutes we're outside the Plaka Hotel, I slide out of his black BMW and watch him drive off, then rush inside to tell Helen the good news.

'I saw you arrive,' she says, coming into the room from the balcony. 'What's happened?'

I grab hold of her. 'It's all over, Helen, we've found the killer.'

Later that day at the Plaka Hotel

'Demos Gramaticos is in police custody,' exclaims Dev, as I open the door to my room. He grabs hold of me and twirls me around.

I laugh. 'So, what was his motive?'

'Demos Gramaticos knew Fivos had overheard him talking, he knew the next time he met James he would tell him who was behind it. That's why they killed him.' He stops for a moment and looks serious. 'James was collateral damage.'

We walk onto the balcony and sit down, he carries on. 'Stamatis was following you in Athens and London, he also drove the car while Gramaticos did the shooting.'

'How do you know all this?'

'Stamatis is spilling the beans, they all do this, he wants a lighter sentence.'

'And Gramaticos?'

'Gramaticos is saying Alex ordered him to do it.' Then as if reading my mind he quickly adds. 'Don't worry about Alex, he has the best legal team in the country. Gramaticos has a history of violence...' He stops and looks at me. 'He's safely behind bars, he won't be calling you again.'

I sigh with relief. Maybe this is the wake-up call Alex needs to get his life in order.

41

Plaka Hotel
8.00 am in the morning

Helen took me by surprise last night, she booked us flights back to London. I know I have to get back to work, and I know she needs to do things in London, but I thought we'd have a few more days in Athens.

I called Dev and told him, he sounded a bit surprised, said he'd pop round in the morning to see us before we leave for the airport, he said if he has time he'll drive us there so I'm sat here with Helen waiting for him.

Helen looks at her watch, then at me.

My phone rings, it's Dev.

A minute later I put the phone down.

She looks at me expectantly.

'He's very busy, he can't come round at the moment.'

'Okay, then we'll get a cab to the airport, we don't want to miss our flight, do we?'

As we enter Athens Eleftherios Venizelos airport, I feel flat and empty, I should feel happy, but I don't.

'Beth!'

I turn, it's Dev.

He rushes over, kisses Helen on both cheeks, then does the same to me.

I swallow and bite down hard on my lip. I've grown to like him a lot, what a shame he doesn't live in London. He looks pale and tired, his blue eyes rest on my face briefly and he smiles.

'Have a good journey, come back soon.'

I nod and smile, then turn to catch up with Helen, she's a few steps ahead of me heading towards check-in.

'Cheer up,' she mutters, grabbing my arm and pulling me along with her. 'We might be going to Spain for Easter.'

I try to smile but I can't.

She glances back at Dev, who's still watching us. 'He's a loner Beth. He used to be married but since his divorce he's never had a permanent relationship. James said he was worried about him.'

She looks at me to make sure I'm taking it in then carries on. 'Many women find him attractive, the problem is he doesn't stay with them for long.'

I have a sudden urge to stay, I turn, Dev's still watching me.

Helen grabs my hand. 'Come on, Beth, we'll miss the flight.' She suddenly hugs me. 'Cheer up, I've a feeling he'll be visiting you soon in London.'

THANKS FOR READING...

Because reviews are critical to the success of an author's career, if you enjoyed reading *The Killing*, please consider leaving a review or rating on Amazon.

Just a short sentence makes a huge difference. Reviews and ratings increase visibility and your help in leaving one will make a huge difference to this author - click here

Thank you for taking the time to read my work.

CARA

PANIC EXTRACT - BOOK 3

LONDON

Dev boards the train, he hates London rush hour, he hasn't taken the train for a while, it hasn't changed, in fact it's worse than it used to be. More people and the noise, he thought Athens was bad but this train is a joke, it's more like a cattle carrier.

He moves slowly along to allow a woman with a rucksack some room, she turns and knocks him with it, he curses under his breath, she smiles shyly.

This is another of his pet peeves, why do they bring them on trains, with the amount of people living in London there isn't room for the bloody things.

Suddenly his body tenses, nobody else has noticed him, but he has, it's the sort of thing he does, he's trained in these things. The guy looks normal, blue sweatshirt, blue jeans, hat pulled down... but the guy's sweating, he has a rucksack in front of him, he's looking wildly around, muttering to himself, his hands tremble.

How can I get to him when I'm knee deep in people?

He starts edging his way slowly towards the guy. He's two feet away, people are glaring at him as he pushes past them.

The guy hasn't noticed him, he keeps his head down, must not alert him. Three people in front of him are blocking his way. Trying to be as calm as he can be he pushes past them, the seconds are ticking by, he has to make it before the doors close.

He's right up to him, the guy turns his head and sees him.

Is he going to detonate it now? Shit his hand's going inside the rucksack.

With an almighty push Dev grabs the guy's hand, the guy grimaces, tries to push him away.

Doors slam shut – fear on faces around them – people instinctively try to push back from them.

The cocky little bastard tries to kick his shin, there's pure hatred in his sparkling black eyes. Dev has the guy's hand in a lock, but he's struggling to get away.

The train races through the tunnel then starts slowing down, they're entering Marble Arch Tube station.

With the full force of his body locking the guy to the tube door, he moves his other hand to grip his wrist, now he can't get away.

The smell of fear is all around the carriage, it's so quiet you could hear a pin drop.

What happens if the guy falls out of the train when the doors open, will it detonate whatever shit he's carrying?

The train squeals into the station.

Not a sound in the carriage.

Doors open – Dev leaps out dragging the guy with him, one hand holding his wrist the other around his neck. The guy's kicking and screaming, everyone stands looking terrified.

Next minute station security is all over the place, pushing past passengers.

Strong arms are on the would-be bomber, while others gently take away the rucksack.

Dev pulls out his phone and texts:

Suicide bomber stopped - Marble Arch Tube.

Suddenly there's a piercing scream.

'Alluha Akbar – infidels! We have more, you stopped me, but you can't stop us all.'

He's carried away screaming by armed police, special agents arrive to cordon off the area and dismantle the bomb.

PAYBACK BOOK 4

A GRIPPING FAST-PACED ROMANTIC SUSPENSE THRILLER…

BETH DOESN'T GO LOOKING for trouble, but trouble always seems to find her...

She's no stranger to the seedier side of life but this time she's stretched to the limit both emotionally and physically.

In one hell of a journey through Granada and southern Spain, Beth's confronted by ruthless drug and people traffickers.

As her every move is watched, she travels to the drug capital of Spain to rescue friends from a vicious kingpin of the drug and sex trade.

PAYBACK IS a gripping fast-paced romantic suspense thriller set in stunning locations with characters you'll love!

PURE EVIL BOOK 5

BETH'S BACK AT WORK BUT SHE'S REPORTING ON CRIME NOT POLITICS...

PURE EVIL - Available on Amazon

HER BOSS SAYS he'll ease her in gently but that's not what happens when a dead body's discovered.

Then a shooting takes place outside a casino in London's Mayfair.

Beth's now caught up in the dark and seedy underbelly of London's West End plus she's still struggling emotionally with the events that happened in Spain.

PURE EVIL is a gripping fast-paced edge of your seat thriller with old and new characters you'll love, perfect for fans of Robert Galbraith and LJ Ross.

FALLOUT BOOK 6

BETH'S BACK ON THE BEAT IN ANOTHER FAST-PACED THRILLER SET IN LONDON...

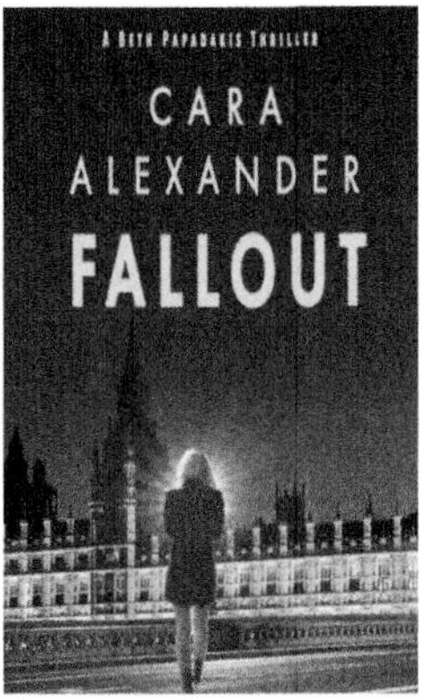

She's asked to cover a terrorist attack with her colleague but things go terribly wrong in more ways than one...

Was it an inside job? Is there a mole in Westminster?

Then a detective's found dead - did he have links to organized crime?

And why doesn't her boss let her cover the story?

While all this is happening Dev drops a bombshell which puts her life in turmoil.

FATAL INTENT BOOK 7

BETH'S BACK ON THE CRIME BEAT IN THIS DARK, FAST-PACED CRIME THRILLER.

She's sent to cover a potential serial killer case in north London. Two women murdered already - is there going to be a third?

Her colleague Fred's sent to cover a hotel killing in London's Piccadilly, which could be disastrous for him.

In the meantime, Dev, who works for MI6, is being transferred to the Middle East.

He asked Beth to go with him - he's still waiting for an answer - how long will he wait?

FOLLOWED BOOK 1

A GRIPPING FAST PACED THRILLER...

Beth's hopes of starting a new life in London come crashing down when on her way home from an interview she's attacked. She fights him off, but that's not the end of it...she's being followed.

Is there a stalker in the small village where it happened?

She meets an old friend from school who still lives in the village and now works for the police. He offers to help, but is he really trying to help, or does he have other things on his mind - she knows he always liked her.

Much later Beth discovers a web of corruption the tentacles of which stretch much further than the small village in the Cotswolds.

***FOLLOWED* is a gripping fast paced thriller that will keep you on the edge of your seat.**

BETH PAPADAKIS BOXSET 1-3

FOLLOWED : THE KILLING : PANIC

FREE in Kindle Unlimited!

FREE BOOK GIVEAWAY

Visit my website at **www.caraaalexander.com** and sign up to my VIP Club to receive a FREE digital copy of BREAKUP the prequel to the Beth Papadakis crime series and be the first to receive news and previews of forthcoming works.

Never miss a new release.

I usually email once a month unless I have something really good to tell you.

No spam, ever, guaranteed. You can unsubscribe at any time.

ABOUT THE AUTHOR

I write fast-paced edge of your seat thrillers with a pinch of romance which I hope you enjoy reading as much as I do writing them.

At the moment, I live in London but I've lived in Spain and Greece which are the backdrops of some of the Beth Papadakis books.

If you have any comments or questions about the books please contact me. I love getting feedback, and reply as quickly as possible. I look forward to seeing you on the inside of my VIP readers' club.

You can visit my website at...

https://www.caraaalexander.com

Facebook.com/caraalexanderauthor

CARA

For my Family with love

Printed in Great Britain
by Amazon

30309935R00152